The Ray of Displacement
and other stories

By

Harriet Prescott Spofford

British Library Cataloguing-in-Publication Data
A catalogue record for this book is available from the
British Library

Harriet Elizabeth Prescott Spofford

Harriet Elizabeth Prescott Spofford was born on 3rd April 1835 in Calais, Maine, United States. She is now best known for her novels, poems and detective stories – a true pioneer of the American detective genre. When she was still a baby, Spofford's parents moved to Newburyport, Massachusetts, where she chose to stay for almost her entire life. Although she spent many of her winters in Boston and Washington D.C., Newburyport remained always close to Spofford's heart.

She attended the Putnam Free School in Newburyport and Pinkerton Academy in Derry, New Hampshire from 1853 to 1855. At Newburyport her prize essay on Hamlet drew the attention of Thomas Wentworth Higginson (a Unitarian minister, author, abolitionist, and soldier), who soon became her friend and gave Spofford much needed counsel and encouragement throughout her career. When Spofford was in her mid-twenties, her parents suffered from ill health, and of necessity she was set to work as a writer, sometimes labouring fifteen hours a day. She contributed to various Boston story papers for small fees, but her first major success came in 1859; this was Spofford's submission to *Atlantic Monthly* (a literary and cultural magazine) of a story about Parisian life, 'In a Cellar'. The magazine's editor, James Russell Lowell, first believed the story to be a translation and withheld it from publication. Reassured it was original, he eventually published it, and the narrative established her reputation. After this success, Spofford became a welcome contributor to the chief periodicals of the United States, both of prose and poetry.

Spofford's fiction had very little in common with what was regarded as representative of 'the New England mind.' Her **gothic romances** were set apart by luxuriant descriptions and an unconventional handling of female **stereotypes** of the day. Her writing was ideal and intense in feeling, revelling in sensuous delights and material splendour. Nowhere was this more evident than, in 'Circumstance', an allegorical short story which takes place in the woods of Maine. In this tale, the protagonist comes into contact with the Indian Devil, forcing her to come to terms with her own life, sexuality and fears. When Wentworth Higginson asked Emily Dickinson whether she had read Spofford's work, Dickinson replied, 'I read Miss Prescott's **'Circumstance,'** but it followed me in the dark, so I avoided her.' Other notable works include *The Thief in the Night* (1872), *The Servant Girl Question* (1881), *A Scarlet Poppy and Other Stories* (1894), and *The Fairy Changeling* (1910).

In 1865, at the age of thirty, the authoress married Richard S. Spofford, a Boston lawyer, and the couple resided on Deer Island overlooking the **Merrimack River** at **Amesbury**, a suburb of Newburyport. They lived here for the rest of their lives. Harriet Prescott Spofford died on 14th August 1921, aged eighty-six.

TABLE OF CONTENTS

THE RAY

OF

DISPLACEMENT

"We should have to reach the Infinite to arrive at the Impossible."

IT would interest none but students should I recite the circumstances of the discovery. Prosecuting my usual researches, I seemed rather to have stumbled on this tremendous thing than to have evolved it from formulæ.

Of course, you already know that all molecules, all atoms, are separated from each other by spaces perhaps as great, when compared relatively, as those which separate the members of the stellar universe. And when by my Y-ray I could so far increase these spaces that I could pass one solid body through another, owing to the differing situation of their atoms, I felt no disembodied spirit had wider, freer range than I. Until my discovery was made public my power over the material universe was practically unlimited.

Le Sage's theory concerning ultra-mundane corpuscles was rejected because corpuscles could not pass through solids. But here were corpuscles passing through solids. As I proceeded, I found that at the displacement of one one-billionth of a centimeter the object capable of passing through another was still visible, owing to the refraction of the air, and had the power of communicating its polarization; and that at two one-billionths the object became invisible, but that at either displacement the subject, if a person, could see into the present plane; and all movement and direction were voluntary. I further found my Y-ray could so polarize a substance that its touch in turn temporarily polarized anything with which it came in contact, a negative current moving atoms to the left, and a positive to the right of the present plane.

My first experience with this new principle would have made a less determined man drop the affair. Brant had been by way of dropping into my office and laboratory when in town. As I afterwards recalled, he showed a signal interest in certain toxicological experiments. "Man alive!" I had said to him once, "let those crystals alone! A single one of them will send you where you never see the sun!" I was uncertain if he brushed one off the slab. He did not return for some months. His wife, as I heard afterwards, had a long and baffling illness in the meantime, divorcing him on her recovery; and he had remained out of sight, at last leaving his native place for the great city. He had come in now, plausibly to ask my opinion of a stone--a diamond of unusual size and water.

I put the stone on a glass shelf in the next room while looking for the slide. You can imagine my sensation when that diamond, with something like a flash of shadow, so intense and swift it was, burst into a hundred rays of blackness and subsided--a pile of carbon! I had forgotten that the shelf happened to be negatively polarized, consequently everything it touched sharing its polarization, and that in pursuing my experiment I had polarized myself also, but with the opposite current; thus the atoms of my fingers passing through the spaces of the atoms of the stone already polarized, separated them negatively so far that they suffered disintegration and returned to the normal. "Good heavens! What has happened!" I cried before I thought. In a moment he was in the rear room and bending with me over the carbon. "Well," he said straightening himself directly, "you gave me a pretty fright. I thought for a moment that was my diamond."

"But it is!" I whispered.

"Pshaw!" he exclaimed roughly. "What do you take me for? Come, come, I'm not here for tricks. That's enough damned legerdemain. Where's my diamond?"

With less dismay and more presence of mind I should have edged along to my batteries, depolarized myself, placed in vacuum the tiny shelf of glass and applied my Y-ray; and with, I knew not what, of convulsion and flame the atoms might have slipped into place. But, instead, I stood gasping. He turned and surveyed me; the low order of his intelligence could receive but one impression.

"Look here," he said, "you will give me back my stone! Now! Or I will have an officer here!"

My mind was flying like the current through my coils. How could I restore the carbon to its original, as I must, if at all, without touching it, and how could I gain time without betraying my secret? "You are avery short," I said. "What would you do with your officer?"

"Give you up! Give you up, appear against you, and let you have a sentence of twenty years behind bars."

"Hard words, Mr. Brant. You could say I had your property. I could deny it. Would your word outweigh mine? But return to the office in five minutes--if it is a possible thing you shall--"

"And leave you to make off with my jewel! Not by a long shot! I'm a bad man to deal with, and I'll have my stone or--"

"Go for your officer," said I.

His eye, sharp as a dagger's point, fell an instant. How could he trust me? I might escape with my booty. Throwing open the window to call, I might pinion him from behind, powerful as he was. But before he could gainsay, I had taken half a dozen steps backward, reaching my batteries.

"Give your alarm," I said. I put out my hand, lifting my lever, turned the current into my coils, and blazed up my Y-ray for half a heart- beat, succeeding in that brief time in reversing and in receiving the current that so far changed matters that the thing I touched would remain normal, although I was left still so far subjected to the ray of the less displacement that I ought, when the thrill had subsided, to be able to step through the wall as easily as if no wall were there. "Do you see what I have here?" I most unwisely exclaimed. "In one second I could annihilate you--" I had no time for more, or even to make sure I was correct, before, keeping one eye on me, he had called the officer.

"Look here," he said again, turning on me. "I know enough to see you have something new there, some of your damned inventions. Come, give me my diamond, and if it is worth while I'll find the capital, go halves, and drop this matter."

"Not to save your life!" I cried.

"You know me, officer," he said, as the blue coat came running in. "I give this man into custody for theft."

"It is a mistake, officer," I said. "But you will do your duty."

"Take him to the central station," said Mr. Brant, "and have him searched. He has a jewel of mine on his person."

"Yer annar's sure it's not on the primmises?" asked the officer.

"He has had no time--"

"Sure, if it's quick he do be he's as like to toss it in a corner--"

I stretched out my hand to a knob that silenced the humming among my wires, and at the same time sent up a thread of white fire whose instant rush and subsidence hinted of terrible power behind. The last divisible particle of radium--their eyeballs throbbed for a week.

"Search," I said. "But be careful about shocks. I don't want murder here, too."

Apparently they also were of that mind. For, recovering their sight, they threw my coat over my shoulders and marched me between them to the station, where I was searched, and, as it was already late, locked into a cell for the night.

I could not waste strength on the matter. I was waiting for the dead middle of the night. Then I should put things to proof.

I confess it was a time of intense breathlessness while waiting for silence and slumber to seal the world. Then I called upon my soul, and I stepped boldly forward and walked through that stone wall as if it had been air.

Of course, at my present displacement I was perfectly visible, and I slipped behind this and that projection, and into that alley, till sure of safety. There I made haste to my quarters, took the shelf holding the carbon, and at once subjected it to the necessary treatment. I was unprepared for the result. One instant the room seemed full of a blinding white flame, an intolerable heat, which shut my eyes and singed my hair and blistered my face.

"It is the atmosphere of a fire-dissolving planet," I thought. And then there was darkness and a strange odor.

I fumbled and stumbled about till I could let in the fresh air; and presently I saw the dim light of the street lamp. Then I turned on my own lights--and there was the quartz slab with a curious fusing of its edges, and in the center, flashing, palpitating, lay the diamond, all fire and whiteness. I wonder if it were not considerably larger; but it was hot as if just fallen from Syra Vega; it contracted slightly after subjection to dephlogistic gases.

It was near morning when, having found Brant's address, I passed into his house and his room, and took my bearings. I found his waistcoat, left the diamond in one of its pockets, and returned. It would not do to remain away, visible or invisible. I must be vindicated, cleared of the charge, set right before the world by Brant's appearing and confessing his mistake on finding the diamond in his pocket.

Judge Brant did nothing of the kind. Having visited me in my cell and in vain renewed his request to share in the invention which the habit of his mind convinced him must be of importance, he appeared against me. And the upshot of the business was that I went to prison for the term of years he had threatened.

I asked for another interview with him; but was refused, unless on the terms already declined. My lawyer, with the prison chaplain, went to him, but to no purpose. At last I went myself, as I had gone before, begging him not to ruin the work of my life. He regarded me as a bad dream, and I could not undeceive him without betraying my secret. I returned to my cell and again waited. For to escape was only to prevent possible vindication. If Mary had lived--but I was alone in the world.

The chaplain arranged with my landlord to take a sum of money I had, and to keep my rooms and apparatus intact till the expiration of my sentence. And then I put on the shameful and degrading prison garb and submitted to my fate.

It was a black fate. On the edge of the greatest triumph over matter that had ever been achieved, on the verge of announcing the actuality of the Fourth Dimension of Space, and of defining and declaring its laws, I was a convict laborer at a prison bench.

One day Judge Brant, visiting a client under sentence of death, in relation to his fee, made pretext to look me up, and stopped at my bench. "And how do you like it as far as you've gone?" he said.

"So that I go no farther," I replied. "And unless you become accessory to my taking off, you will acknowledge you found the stone in your pocket--"

"Not yet, not yet," he said, with an unctuous laugh. "It was a keen jest you played. Regard this as a jest in return. But when you are ready, I am ready."

The thing was hopeless. That night I bade good-bye to the life that had plunged me from the pinnacle of light to the depths of hell.

When again conscious I lay on a cot in the prison hospital. My attempt had been unsuccessful. St. Angel sat beside me. It was here, practically, he came into my life--alas! that I came into his.

In the long nights of darkness and failing faintness, when horror had me by the throat, he was beside me, and his warm, human touch was all that held me while I hung over the abyss. When I swooned off again his hand, his voice, his bending face recalled me. "Why not let me go, and then an end?" I sighed.

"To save you from a great sin," he replied. And I clung to his hand with the animal instinct of living.

I was well, and in my cell, when he said. "You claim to be an honest man--"

"And yet?"

"You were about taking that which did not belong to you."

"I hardly understand."

"Can you restore life once taken?"

"Oh, life! That worthless thing!"

"Lent for a purpose."

"For torture!"

"If by yourself you could breathe breath into any pinch of feathers and toss it off your hand a creature-- but, as it is, life is a trust. And you, a man of parts, of power, hold it only to return with usury."

"And stripped of the power of gathering usury! Robbed of the work about to revolutionize the world!"

"The world moves on wide waves. Another man will presently have reached your discovery."

As if that were a thing to be glad of! I learned afterwards that St. Angel had given up the sweetness of life for the sake of his enemy. He had gone to prison, and himself worn the stripes, rather than the woman he loved should know her husband was the criminal.

Perhaps he did not reconcile this with his love of inviolate truth. But St. Angel had never felt so much regard for his own soul as for the service of others. Self-forgetfulness was the dominant of all his nature.

"Tell me," he said, sitting with me, "about your work."

A whim of trustfulness seized me. I drew an outline, but paused at the look of pity on his face. He felt there was but one conclusion to draw--that I was a madman.

"Very well," I said, "you shall see." And I walked through the wall before his amazed eyes, and walked back again.

For a moment speechless, "You have hypnotic power," then he said. "You made me think I saw it."

"You did see it. I can go free any day I choose."

"And you do not?"

"I must be vindicated." And I told exactly what had taken place with Brant and his diamond. "Perhaps that vindication will never come," I said at last. "The offended amour propre, and the hope of gain, hindered in the beginning. Now he will find it impossible."

"That is too monstrous to believe!" said St. Angel. "But since you can, why not spend an hour or two at night with your work?"

"In these clothes! How long before I should be brought back? The first wayfarer--oh, you see!"

St. Angel thought a while. "You are my size," he said then. "We will exchange clothes. I will remain here. In three hours return, that you may get your sleep. It is fortunate the prison should be in the same town."

Night after night then I was in my old rooms, the shutters up, lost in my dreams and my researches, arriving at great ends.

Night after night I reappeared on the moment, and St. Angel went his way.

I had now found that molecular displacement can be had in various directions. Going further, I saw that gravity acts on bodies whose molecules are on the same plane, and one of the possible results of the application of the Y-ray was the suspension of the laws of gravity. This possibly accounted for an almost inappreciable buoyancy and the power of directing one's course. My last studies showed that a substance thus treated has the degenerative power of attracting the molecules of any norm into its new orbit--a disastrous possibility. A chair might disappear into a table previously treated by a Y-ray. In fact, the outlook was to infinity. The change so slight--the result so astonishing! The subject might go into molecular interstices as far removed, to all essential purpose, as if billions of miles away in interstellar space. Nothing was changed, nothing disrupted; but the thing had stepped aside to let the world go by. The secrets of the world were mine. The criminal was at my mercy. The lover had no reserves from me. And as for my enemy, the Lord had delivered him into my hand. I could leave him only a puzzle for the dissectors. I could make him, although yet alive, a conscious ghost to stand or wander in his altered shape through years of nightmare alone and lost. What wonders of energy would follow this ray of displacement. What withdrawal of malignant growth and deteriorating tissue was to come. "To what heights of succor for humanity the surgeon can rise with it!" said St. Angel, as, full of my enthusiasm, I dilated on the marvel.

"He can work miracles!" I exclaimed. "He can heal the sick, walk on the deep, perhaps--who knows--raise the dead!"

I was at the height of my endeavor when St. Angel brought me my pardon. He had so stated my case to the Governor, so spoken of my interrupted career, and of my prison conduct, that the pardon had been given. I refused to accept it. "I accept," I said, "nothing but vindication, if I stay here till the day of judgment!"

"But there is no provision for you now," he urged. "Officially you no longer exist."

"Here I am," I said, "and here I stay."

"At any rate," he continued, "come out with me now and see the Governor, and see the world and the daylight outdoors, and be a man among men a while!"

With the stipulation that I should return, I put on a man's clothes again and went out the gates.

It was with a thrill of exultation that, exhibiting the affairs in my room to St. Angel, finally I felt the vibrating impulse that told me I had received the ray of the larger displacement. In a moment I should be viewless as the air.

"Where are you?" said St. Angel, turning this way and that. "What has become of you?"

"Seeing is believing," I said. "Sometimes not seeing is the naked truth."

"Oh, but this is uncanny!" he exclaimed. "A voice out of empty air."

"Not so empty! But place your hand under the second coil. Have no fear. You hear me now," I said. "I am in perhaps the Fourth Dimension. I am invisible to any one not there--to all the world, except, presently, yourself. For now you, you also, pass into the unseen. Tell me what you feel."

"Nothing," he said. "A vibration--a suspicion of one. No, a blow, a sense of coming collapse, so instant it has passed."

"Now," I said, "there is no one on earth with eyes to see you but myself!"

"That seems impossible."

"Did you see me? But now you do. We are on the same plane. Look in that glass. There is the reflection of the room, of the window, the chair. Do you see me? Yourself?"

"Powers of the earth and air, but this is ghastly!" said St. Angel.

"It is the working of natural law. Now we will see the world, ourselves unseen."

"An unfair advantage."

"Perhaps. But there are things to accomplish to-day." What things I never dreamed; or I had stayed on the threshold.

I wanted St. Angel to know the manner of man this Brant was. We went out, and arrested our steps only inside Brant's office.

"This door is always blowing open!" said the clerk, and he returned to a woman standing in a suppliant attitude. "The Judge has gone to the races," he said, "and he's left word that Tuesday morning your goods'll be put out of the house if you don't pay up!" The woman went her way weeping.

Leaving, we mounted a car; we would go to the races ourselves. I doubt if St. Angel had ever seen anything of the sort. I observed him quietly slip a dime into the conductor's pocket--he felt that even the invisible, like John Gilpin, carried a right. "This opens a way for the right hand undreamed of the left," he said to me later.

It was not long before we found Judge Brant, evidently in an anxious frame, his expanse of countenance white with excitement. He had been plunging heavily, as I learned, and had big money staked, not upon the favorite but upon Hannan, the black mare. "That man would hardly put up so much on less than a certainty," I thought. Winding our way unseen among the grooms and horses, I found what I suspected--a plan to pocket the favorite. "But I know a game worth two of that," I said. I took a couple of small smooth pebbles, previously prepared, from the chamois bag into which I had put them with some others and an aluminum wafer treated for the larger displacement, and slipped one securely under the favorite's saddle-girth. When he warmed to his work he should be, for perhaps half an hour, at the one-billionth point, before the virtue expired, and capable of passing through every obstacle as he was directed.

"Hark you, Danny," then I whispered in the jockey's ear.

"Who are you? What--I--I--don't--" looking about with terror.

"It's no ghost," I whispered hurriedly. "Keep your nerve. I am flesh and blood--alive as you. But I have the property which for half an hour I give you--a new discovery. And knowing Bub and Whittler's game, it's up to you to knock 'em out. Now, remember, when they try the pocket ride straight through them!"

Other things kept my attention; and when the crucial moment came I had some excited heart-beats. And so had Judge Brant. It was in the instant when Danny, having held the favorite well in hand for the first stretch, Hannan and Darter in the lead and the field following, was about calling on her speed, that suddenly Bub and Whittler drew their horses' heads a trifle more closely together, in such wise that it was impossible to pass on either side, and a horse could no more shoot ahead than if a stone wall stood there. "Remember, Danny!" I shouted, making a trumpet of my hands. "Ride straight through!"

And Danny did. He pulled himself together, and set his teeth as if it were a compact with powers of evil, and rode straight through without turning a hair, or disturbing either horse or rider. Once more the Y- ray was triumphant.

But about Judge Brant the air was blue. It would take a very round sum of money to recoup the losses of those few moments. I disliked to have St. Angel hear him; but it was all in the day's work.

The day had not been to Judge Brant's mind, as at last he bent his steps to the club. As he went it occurred to me to try upon him the larger ray of displacement, and I slipped down the back of his collar the wafer I had ready. He would not at once feel its action, but in the warmth either of walking or dining, its properties should be lively for nearly an hour. I had curiosity to see if the current worked not only through all substances, but through all sorts and conditions.

"I should prefer a better pursuit," said St. Angel, as we reached the street. "Is there not something ignoble in it?"

"In another case. Here it is necessary to hound the criminal, to see the man entirely. A game not to be played too often, for there is work to be done before establishing the counteracting currents that may ensure reserves and privacies to people. To-night let us go to the club with Judge Brant, and then I will back to my cell."

As you may suppose, Brant was a man neither of imagination nor humor. As you have seen, he was hard and cruel, priding himself on being a good hater, which in his contention meant indulgence of a preternaturally vindictive temper when prudence allowed. With more cunning than ability, he had achieved some success in his profession, and he secured admission to a good club, recently crowning his efforts, when most of the influential members were absent, by getting himself made one of its governors.

It would be impossible to find a greater contrast to this wretch than in St. Angel--a man of delicate imagination and pure fancy, tender to the child on the street, the fly on the wall; all his atmosphere that of kindness. Gently born, but too finely bred, his physical resistance was so slight that his immunity lay in not being attacked. His clean, fair skin, his brilliant eyes, spoke of health, but the fragility of frame did not speak of strength. Yet St. Angel's life was the active principle of good; his neighborhood was purification.

I was revolving these things while we followed Judge Brant, when I saw him pause in an agitated manner, like one startled out of sleep. A quick shiver ran over his strong frame; he turned red and pale, then with a shrug went on. The displacement had occurred. He was now on the plane of invisibility, and we must have a care ourselves.

Wholly unconscious of any change, the man pursued his way. The street was as usual. There was the boy who always waited for him with the extra but to-night was oblivious; and failing to get his attention the Judge walked on. A shower that had been threatening began to fall, the sprinkle becoming a downpour, with umbrellas spread and people hurrying. The Judge hailed a car; but the motorman was as blind as the newsboy. The shower stopped as suddenly as it had begun, but he went on some paces before perceiving that he was perfectly dry, for as he shut and shook his umbrella not a drop fell, and as he took off his hat and looked at it, not an atom of moisture was to be found there. Evidently bewildered, and looking about shamefacedly, I fancied I could hear him saying, with his usual oaths, "I must be deucedly overwrought, or this is some blue devilment."

As the Judge took his accustomed seat in the warm and brilliantly lighted room, and picking up the evening paper, looked over the columns, the familiar every-day affair quieting his nerves so that he could have persuaded himself he had been half asleep as he walked, he was startled by the voice, not four feet away, of one of the old officers who made the Kings County their resort. Something had ruffled the doughty hero. "By the Lord Harry, sir," he was saying in unmodulated tones, "I should like to know what this club is coming to when you can spring on it the election of such a man as this Brant! Judge? What's he Judge of? Beat his wife, too, didn't he? The governors used to be gentlemen!"

"But you know, General," said his vis-à-vis, "I think no more of him than you do; but when a man lives at the Club--"

"Lives here!" burst in the other angrily. "He hasn't anywhere else to live! Is there a decent house in town open to him? Well, thank goodness, I've somewhere else to go before he comes in! The sight of him gives me a fit of the gout!" And the General stumped out stormily.

"Old boy seems upset!" said some one not far away. "But he's right. It was sheer impudence in the fellow to put up his name."

I could see Brant grow white and gray with anger, as surprised and outraged, wondering what it meant--if the General intended insult--if Scarsdale--but no, apparently they had not seen him. The contemptuous words rankled; the sweat stood on his forehead.

Had not the moment been serious, there were a thousand tricks to play. But the potency of the polarization was subsiding and in a short time the normal molecular plane would be re-established. It was there that I made my mistake. I should not have allowed him to depolarize so soon. I should have kept him bewildered and foodless till famished and weak. Instead, as ion by ion the effect of the ray decreased, his shape grew vague and misty, and then one and another man there rubbed his eyes, for Judge Brant was sitting in his chair and a waiter was hastening towards him.

It had all happened in a few minutes. Plainly the Judge understood nothing of the circumstances. He was dazed, but he must put the best face on it; and he ordered his dinner and a pony of brandy, eating like a hungry animal.

He rose, after a time, refreshed, invigorated, and all himself. Choosing a cigar, he went into another room, seeking a choice lounging place, where for a while he could enjoy his ease and wonder if anything worse than a bad dream had befallen. As for the General's explosion, it did not signify; he was conscious of such opinion; he was overliving it; he would be expelling the old cock yet for conduct unbecoming a gentleman.

Meanwhile, St. Angel, tiring of the affair, and weary, had gone into this room, and in an arm-chair by the hearth was awaiting me--the intrusive quality of my observations not at all to his mind. He had eaten nothing all day, and was somewhat faint. He had closed his eyes, and perhaps fallen into a light doze when he must have been waked by the impact of Brant's powerful frame, as the latter took what seemed to him the empty seat. I expected to see Brant at once flung across the rug by St. Angel's natural effort in rising. Instead, Brant sank into the chair as into down pillows.

I rushed, as quickly as I could, to seize and throw him off, "Through him! Pass through him! Come out!

Come to me!" I cried. And people to- day remember that voice out of the air, in the Kings County Club.

It seemed to me that I heard a sound, a sob, a whisper, as if one cried with a struggling sigh, "Impossible!" And with that a strange trembling convulsed Judge Brant's great frame, he lifted his hands, he thrust out his feet, his head fell forward, he groaned gurglingly, shudder after shudder shook him as if every muscle quivered with agony or effort, the big veins started out as if every pulse were a red-hot iron. He was wrestling with something, he knew not what, something as antipathetic to him as white is to black; every nerve was concentrated in rebellion, every fiber struggled to break the spell.

The whole affair was that of a dozen heart-beats--the attempt of the opposing molecules each to draw the other into its own orbit. The stronger physical force, the greater aggregation of atoms was prevailing. Thrust upward for an instant, Brant fell back into his chair exhausted, the purple color fading till his face shone fair as a girl's, sweet and smiling as a child's, white as the face of a risen spirit--Brant's!

Astounded, I seized his shoulder and whirled him about. There was no one else in the chair. I looked in every direction. There was no St. Angel to be seen. There was but one conclusion to draw--the molecules of Brant's stronger material frame had drawn into their own plane the molecules of St. Angel's.

I rushed from the place, careless if seen or unseen, howling in rage and misery. I sought my laboratory, and in a fiend's fury depolarized myself, and I demolished every instrument, every formula, every vestige of my work. I was singed and scorched and burned, but I welcomed any pain. And I went back to prison, admitted by the officials who hardly knew what else to do. I would stay there, I thought, all my days. God grant they should be few! It would be seen that a life of imprisonment and torture were too little punishment for the ruin I had wrought.

It was after a sleepless night, of which every moment seemed madness, that, the door of my cell opening, I saw St. Angel. St. Angel? God have mercy on me, no, it was Judge Brant I saw!

He came forward, with both hands extended, a grave, imploring look on his face. "I have come," he said, a singular sweet overtone in his voice that I had never heard before, yet which echoed like music in my memory, "to make you all the reparation in my power. I will go with you at once before the Governor, and acknowledge that I have found the diamond. I can never hope to atone for what you have suffered. But as long as I live, all that I have, all that I am, is yours!"

There was a look of absolute sweetness on his face that for a dizzy moment made me half distraught. "We will go together," he said. "I have to stop on the way and tell a woman whose mortgage comes due to- day that I have made a different disposition; and, do you know," he added brightly, after an instant's hesitation, "I think I shall help her pay it!" and he laughed gayly at the jest involved.

"Will you say that you have known my innocence all these years?" I said sternly.

"Is not that," he replied, with a touching and persuasive quality of tone, "a trifle too much? Do you think this determination has been reached without a struggle? If you are set right before the world, is not something due to--Brant?"

"If I did not know who and what you are," I said, "I should think the soul of St. Angel had possession of you!"

The man looked at me dreamily. "Strange!" he murmured. "I seem to have heard something like that before. However," as if he shook off a perplexing train of thought, "all that is of no consequence. It is not who you are, but what you do. Come, my friend, don't deny me, don't let the good minute slip. Surely the undoing of the evil of a lifetime, the turning of that force to righteousness, is work outweighing all a prison chaplain's--"

My God, what had the intrusion of my incapable hands upon forbidden mysteries done!

"Come," he said. "We will go together. We will carry light into dark places--there are many waiting--"

"St. Angel!" I cried, with a loud voice, "are you here?"

And again the smile of infinite sweetness illuminated the face even as the sun shines up from the depths of a stagnant pool.

THE NEMESIS

OF

MOTHERHOOD

"There are two moments in a diver's life: One, when a beggar he prepares to plunge, One, when a prince he rises with his pearl. Festus, I plunge."--Browning.

Chapter I

THE hospital of the prison was little more than a whitewashed corridor with bald daylight coming through the high gratings. The nurse was neither soft-footed nor soft-hearted.

But the woman occupying one of the cots there was as oblivious of outer circumstances as if she were in the middle of a cloud. It was, in fact, thick cloud that swathed her, body and soul, in black shadow, as she lay there with her baby three days old. If she herself had ever been fair to see, there was small reason to suspect the possibility now; and the little dark atom of humanity she held would perhaps have given any but its mother a feeling of repulsion.

She had been sentenced to a term of years at hard labor for her crime. Although a young woman, she was an old offender. It was held among the officials that there was nothing so bad or so vile that she might not be a part of its wickedness. She had lived on the plane of an animal, an exceedingly cunning and rather vicious animal. Her memories, could she have awakened them, would have revolted any listener however abandoned, and have hardened the heart of an angel.

Yet as she lay there and felt the little new being at her breast, two great tears welled from under her closed eyelids and paused upon her cheeks; a sunbeam through the grating touched them and painted in them the reflection of all heaven. The nurse saw the sunbeam, and drew the shade down; no one looked for any reflection of heaven in that woman's tears.

She was suffering little from her physical troubles, although prostrate from weakness. She knew that everything was wrong with her; but that did not trouble her; she had been in hell too long, she would have said, to fear now; and, to her, death, not birth, seemed a sleep and a forgetting. But through all her varied experience, this was her first child; and the condition where she found herself was a new hell, and one undreamed of before. This little creature, drawing her life into itself, was something for which she felt a fierce protecting instinct--an unspeakable and angry need of interposing herself between it and the cruelty of the world. Her child--it was foreordained by fate that it must suffer. Her daughter--there was not power enough in the universe to hinder her from sharing her mother's lot. The child must grow up in the alleys, in the gutters. Her first words would be oaths; little criminals would be her companions; sin must be her daily sight, evil must be her atmosphere; she the bantling of a ribald moment, and by right of descent possessor of her mother's indecency. Wrong would come to her earlier than it had come to herself--she remembered sharply the first stirring of the vicious impulses in herself, the first temptation; the first yielding; the bad, bitter joy; the end in wretchedness, in despair, in ruin. He had gone free-- and where there was one of her there were ten of him--and she felt the multitude of him lying in wait for this girl drawing now from her veins the impulse, the yielding, the riot, the rage; and once more the fierce instinct of protection made her clasp the child so closely that it cried out with a feeble cry.

The nurse came and looked at her curiously and saw the tear and went away. The child dropped off to sleep. But far from sleep was the mother, with a fire ravaging her brain. She saw the way marked out for this child; she saw not only that, but the bleeding feet with which she must tread it.

But yet--it was not impossible--she could be saved from all that. There were people who could take her out and away, who could surround her with the things of a different life--she who was innocent now.

Innocent? Was she innocent, this child born with an injured body, with a diseased soul? No intelligence, no cunning, no benevolence, could evade the inevitable. For what she was, that her child was. You do not gather figs from thistles. What she had made herself, she had made her child; what she had become, that her child became also. In being born, the child became all that. This soft and shapeless lip was ready for the lie; those tiny clutching fingers for the theft; those helpless hands for the secret murder; that body would grow lithe and supple for all sin, and would one day wither in the fire of pain. Born vile, to wallow in slime, the child would take only what was given to it--from the unknown, nameless father corruption; from the mother the blackness of

39

shameless things of midnight. All that the mother had done she would do; all that the mother had suffered she would suffer. Had there been any happiness in her part? Not one jot. The child would live to curse the day she saw the light.

She rose on one arm and looked at it. She laid her thin hand on its thin cheek. Her heart suddenly stood still with a wild, unused sensation--could it be love for the child? She fell back on her pillow a chill sweat of horror covering her. All this evil she had given her child in giving it life.

There was something else she could give it.

In the morning the nurse and the doctor could not say that the mother had not overlain the child in sleep. It did not seem best to make any search into the affair, since for this mother's child death was so much better than life.

Chapter II

Every sound in the large and lovely room was muffled by the rich rugs, the silk-hung walls, the heavy curtains. A fire burnt low on the hearth and sent a ruby shadow here and there, flickering over the alabaster vase, the ivory carving, the water-color on the panel, the blue silk coverlet and the billowy lace about the bed. The room was full of the fragrance of a hundred roses. An attendant, velvet-shod, carried away a small gold tray with a bowl of china as translucent as a flower; another nurse sat by the fire and dreamed over the pillow that lay across her knee. All seemed well with the young mother; all seemed well with the child.

She rested deep among her pillows, in a sleepy content; but quite determined on no more experience of this sort. Why could not the race have been continued in some other way? It really seemed as if there were some malevolence toward women. How much she had missed since they forbade her to dance or to ride. The idea of her foregoing all her pleasures for this--and life so short at the best! She would be on a horse again the moment she was able, before the frosty weather was all gone. She had lost the Hunt Ball, as it was. Well, here was the heir, anyway; and he would have to do.

A gush of music came through an opening door or window, a thrill of violins and flutes; there was a small and early german in the next house--how vexatious to be here! And all the rehearsals for the theatricals were over without her; and every one had declared there could never be such a Cleopatra as she; and she had ropes and ropes of pearls to wear, and miles of rose-colored gauzes half to hide and half to reveal the rose-colored tights. Very likely there would have been a fuss; but what was the use of being beautiful all to yourself? At all events, the gauzes would do for the skirt-dances they were going to give for the Blenheim Spaniel Hospital.

There would be some cotillions, anyway, before Lent. She hoped she wasn't going to come out of all this with her color gone. And her figure--it would be a pity if the gowns that had just come from Paris shouldn't fit her now. She would have the boxes opened to-morrow and the gowns spread out for inspection--one of them ought to be simply exquisite--cherry-colored satin, the front embroidered with seed- pearls, cut very low, but with a high ruff, and clouds of old Venice point. Lester van Dycke always said when she wore that shade that Watteau should have painted her. Poor Lester--she couldn't understand why there should have been any feeling about that little flirtation; he was only teaching her how to smoke a cigarette like Carmen. And then it was diverting to see just how far you could go and stop. And really she had been awfully hard up when he lost that money to her at poker. Thank goodness, it was all paid back before he was sent off on that whaling voyage to break up his drinking. How people do slip in and out of your life.--What was that woman doing now? Oh, indeed--they needn't bring that baby to her; she didn't want him.

The nurse, a wise woman as nurses were in the days of Pharaoh, turned down the silken sheet and laid on the mother's arm the bundle of soft wool and filmy lace, baring the little pink face. "I never supposed babies looked like that. Isn't he comical? And you needn't think I'm going to nurse him," she meant to say aloud, but really said only to herself. "He can be brought up by hand; or you may get all the foster- mothers you please. I won't be tied down by a chain two or three hours long, and grow a fright into the bargain!"

"We can't let the little man starve," the nurse was saying. "At any rate, just for the present," she urged. "Till the doctor comes again and we can get just what is wanted."

Were all nurses like this? Wasn't she compelling? A sort of civilized She. Well, if she must. But not to keep it up. How absurd! How perfectly ridiculous! But they were not to think she was going on with it and forego the races and the yachting and everything else. "Don't you know," she said in her thoughts to the baby, "that you're dreadfully in my way?"

The baby smiled--the vacuous little grimace of a baby--and opened his eyes. "Dear me," she said. "How interesting! Do you imagine he sees me? Fancy! And look at the fingers--aren't they quite perfect? And his eyes-- why, they're really--just look at the little fine corners! Do you suppose he knows I'm his mother? Oh, I am his mother!" And the little head had snuggled into place. She gazed at him in a bewildered wonder: something seemed to be taking hold of her very heart-strings. Oh, this scrap of a creature was part of her life itself! She had made him! She had struck this spark of a soul into a being! The idea! But why? The dear person had a soul, of course. And she fell to wondering what kind of soul it was. What kind of a soul--why, didn't people say the son was the avatar of the mother? A soul like hers, to be sure. My gracious, what kind of a soul was hers?

It seemed suddenly to be growing black everywhere about her, whether owing to the new sensations and to exhaustion, or to the too illuminating thought. All along the dusky wall she saw written in letters of flame, Mene, mene, tekel upharsin. She half laughed to think it should be in plain, every-day characters instead of Persian script. Thou art weighed in the balance--and found wanting.

What did it mean? What was weighed? What was found wanting? And what was this blackness? Was she fainting? Or, oh, was she dying!

Heavens! Was this dying? Was she sinking, failing, letting go of life? Don't let her die! Oh, don't let her die! She didn't want to leave all these pleasant things. She was afraid. For, oh, she was not fit to die! She must have made some exclamation, for the nurse was sprinkling her face. "It is all right," the woman was saying. "She is coming to. It's not unusual." Yes; it was no longer black about her: she was in the middle of a great light; she seemed to be withering in it, like a leaf in the fire. In the middle of the great light she saw herself for what she was. In that unknown and vast beyond, her little worthless soul would be lost. That was the kind of soul she had--a little, worthless, paltering one.

That was the kind of soul, then, she had given to her boy. He was to grow up in this great moving world as trifling, as light-minded, as slight as she, she who cared only for the pleasures that waste the body and starve the soul! His little velvet cheek lay on her breast-- oh, how dear he was; how sweet he was, the little new person! And she had made him as useless, as light as a bubble. She recalled a deceit she had practised just before his birth--a scandal she had stimulated; the case that had been laid before her of bringing out a poor man's family for just the money that would buy the emerald cross she wanted, and she had taken refuge behind the immigration laws, and there were the emeralds in her jewel-case; her face burnt to remember the champagne she drank the night she first wore those emeralds--heaven knows what silly things she said! Yes, yes; there was no help for it, this son of hers would want ease, glitter, wine, bibelots! Pleasures that had been follies in her would be follies in him, too, and worse than follies. Her frivolity would be in him effeminacy, her idleness would have made him a voluptuary. He would know nothing and care less for the sin and sorrow on his right hand and his left; he would not waste an hour of his laughing life on any of the grief and pain that made discord in the music. A silken sybarite, he would yield to every temptation;

every gaiety would allure him. The thrones of the world might rock, he would not know it if his clubs were sound. His ambitions would be in his clothes, in his horses. He would have no strength to fight the forces of evil--he would be a part of them. Insufficient, of no purpose in the great scheme of the growth of the race-- oh, was she thinking of her boy, her little son, the dear new, tender life? And then again that sinking, that slipping into outer darkness.

No, no, she must overcome it; she must not die; there was something for her to do; she could not afford to die! She could not have him, when his time came, go out into the dark the trumpery thing she was herself, as he needs must if she did not live to hinder it. He would be without strength to resist the press of evil, for she had given him no strength; he would be without impulse to do good, for she had given him no impulse; he would be without value in the scales of the universe, for she had given him no value. She must live to lead him past the temptation, for she would recognize it; to bid him to see the pitfall; to find, herself, and show to him, the shining mark beyond; to help him in all those straits and perils where being her son, he must otherwise be helpless. That other woman whom the doctor was to bring, that foster-mother, she must go away again. They should give her something for her own baby; but she could not have this one. She might be a better woman; he might draw force and will from her; but from his own mother he would draw love, and the love should keep him safe.

The fire fell, and all was still in the room. The nurse drowsed in her chair. The very roses seemed to hush themselves in dropping now and then a petal lest they wake the mother and the child from their deep, sweet, regenerating sleep.

Chapter III

There was but one room in the log-cabin of the forest clearing. The summer moonlight poured in a flood of pale-green silver through the open door and the windows, glorifying all the place.

The young mother, lying there with her first-born beside her, had done what she could to make the spot homelike till something better should replace it; and it wore a certain reminiscence of castle halls in the tapestry of skins, in the huge antlers, in the crossed arms.

The woman, who had come from a dozen miles away to be with her now-- one to whose help she had gone herself when the forest-fever smote the household there, was in the lean-to with the doctor. The husband was out hunting, unaware of the imminence of the event; and the two lads were with him. There was no one in the room but the mother and her child.

No one? What was this shape in the moonlight--this shining mist--the winged shape of a great angel, gleaming obscurely in the bloom of the broad glow? What the darker shape of another that seemed the shadow of the first? Or were they shapes at all, or more than the phantasmagoria of a failing brain?

She was too weak to note anything closely; but she felt in long thrills through all her frame the soft, slow breathing of the baby at her side, and her soul was full of a rapture of gladness. She felt, moreover, vaguely conscious of a certain dim sense of triumph, for although her father's holdings had gone in a distant branch to the heir male, she knew that she, inheriting of her father, that her son, inheriting of her, truly represented the race- -not that son of many alien mothers who now had name and place.

Left dowerless, through mishap, she had married a man of adventurous spirit, and had come out here, a pioneer, to begin fresh life; her son was to be one of the makers of the new world. But of none of this she thought now or was aware, save as a dull undercurrent. She faintly remembered thinking before he was born that this child was to be the flower of his race; that his mother must make him so; that his mother's father had already made him so--that father in whom there had been no taint of dishonor, of self-seeking, of uncleanness, of distemper of mind or body. Perhaps the nobility had lain dormant in herself; she had feared that; she had tried to rouse it--but on the whole had given herself small time to dwell upon it. There had been far too much to do to think if she possessed virtues and graces. She had had plans, in the early days, of great work among the prisons she would visit, and the help she would give the convict people; of the way in which she would bring pleasure to certain of the insane; and, when war broke out, of the help she might be as an army nurse--she familiar with sick-rooms. But she had had no chance to bring herself to proof; for her father had needed her every hour. And when he had died, she had married a poor man, a prince among poor men as she felt, and she had come out with him to build a new home under new conditions. As, upon the voyage, she had looked over at those in the steerage, her heart had swelled with pity, and with a sense of being in reality one of them, with no right to more ease; she had gone in among them, and an old woman there had died in her arms, and to the child of a poor young wife she had rendered the first offices. And as her foot touched shore her heart had swelled again, but with a sort of ecstasy, thinking of the great promise this land gave to the oppressed of all the earth. On the train across the country she had found two little lads whose people had died and who were bewildered at their homeless condition; and she and her husband had taken them to their home in the wilderness.

Over here life had not been easy; but she had given no sign. It had been beyond her strength; but she had never faltered. She was making home and happiness and she had found a vivid joy in it. She had been lonesome in the long days of necessary solitude; but no one knew it. She had been home-sick for old sights, old faces, old luxuries; but there was always a smile on her lip when any one looked. Sometimes her husband took her with him on his errands to the distant town, and as she saw the busy people going to and fro a great love swept from her to one and all of them. And when her child was coming, she was so glad of him that that love for others seemed only to have opened the way for an inexhaustible fountain of love flowing to him and through him. She had a sort of smiling memory that it took generations to make a gentleman--it had meant generations of mothers, of course; and after all was a gentleman in the first place other than a man of the people who loved his people? Fate must have begun in season with her child. She searched herself, if by mischance any hidden sin in her could come to light in him; she had prayed almost hourly that he might have truth, courage, a pure heart, a generous hand, a selfless spirit, and that, when the ordeal came, if one must go, the child should stay and have his share of the joy of the world that she had found so sweet, unwitting that her very prayer gave him all the loftiness she craved for him.

And now the son had been born to her and slept beside her, a strong and lusty boy, the builder, possibly, of a new race; surely, as she had dreamed, the last richness of an old one. She lay with indistinct, half-wandering fancies, looking into the pouring moonlight. For a moment she was quite sure she saw them--the two great angels; and then the eyelids dropped dreamily, and she saw no more.

"It is a child," said the shadowy angel, hovering over the bed, "whose mother had given him the strength that becomes a man, who has a place to take in the world, a work to do, and a will to do it. The race needs him. He is yours."

"It is a mother," said the shining angel, "who has already given her child the welcome that makes a joyous soul. He shall not miss her smile. He is what she is. He will need love since he will give so much. And she is all compact of love. She is one of the forces of Life. Death, I cannot surrender her."

And the dark angel fled away into the moonlight, and the shining one fanned sleeping mother and child with his wings.

CIRCUMSTANCE

She had remained, during all that day, with a sick neighbor,--those eastern wilds of Maine in that epoch frequently making neighbors and miles synonymous,-- and so busy had she been with care and sympathy that she did not at first observe the approaching night. But finally the level rays, reddening the snow, threw their gleam upon the wall, and, hastily donning cloak and hood, she bade her friends farewell and sallied forth on her return. Home lay some three miles distant, across a copse, a meadow, and a piece of woods,--the woods being a fringe on the skirts of the great forests that stretch far away into the North. That home was one of a dozen log-houses lying a few furlongs apart from each other, with their half-cleared demesnes separating them at the rear from a wilderness untrodden save by stealthy native or deadly panther tribes.

She was in a nowise exalted frame of spirit,--on the contrary, rather depressed by the pain she had witnessed and the fatigue she had endured; but in certain temperaments such a condition throws open the mental pores, so to speak, and renders one receptive of every influence. Through the little copse she walked slowly, with her cloak folded about her, lingering to imbibe the sense of shelter, the sunset filtered in purple through the mist of woven spray and twig, the companionship of growth not sufficiently dense to band against her, the sweet home-feeling of a young and tender wintry wood. It was therefore just on the edge of the evening that she emerged from the place and began to cross the meadow-land. At one hand lay the forest to which her path wound; at the other the evening star hung over a tide of failing orange that slowly slipped down the earth's broad side to sadden other hemispheres with sweet regret. Walking rapidly now, and with her eyes wide-open, she distinctly saw in the air before her what was not there a moment ago, a winding-sheet,--cold, white, and ghastly, waved by the likeness of four wan hands,--that rose with a long inflation, and fell in rigid folds, while a voice, shaping itself from the hollowness above, spectral and melancholy, sighed,-- "The Lord have mercy on the people! The Lord have mercy on the people!" Three times the sheet with its corpse-covering outline waved beneath the pale hands, and the voice, awful in its solemn and mysterious depth, sighed, "The Lord have mercy on the people!" Then all was gone, the place was clear again, the gray sky was obstructed by no deathly blot; she looked about her, shook her shoulders decidedly, and, pulling on her hood, went forward once more.

She might have been a little frightened by such an apparition, if she had led a life of less reality than frontier settlers are apt to lead; but dealing with hard fact does not engender a flimsy habit of mind, and this woman was too sincere and earnest in her character, and too happy in her situation, to be thrown by antagonism, merely, upon superstitious fancies and chimeras of the second-sight. She did not even believe herself subject to an hallucination, but smiled simply, a little vexed that her thought could have framed such a glamour from the day's occurrences, and not sorry to lift the bough of the warder of the woods and enter and disappear in their sombre path. If she had been imaginative, she would have hesitated at her first step into a region whose dangers were not visionary; but I suppose that the thought of a little child at home would conquer that propensity in the most habituated. So, biting a bit of spicy birch, she went along. Now and then she came to a gap where the trees had been partially felled, and here she found that the lingering twilight was explained by that peculiar and perhaps electric film which sometimes sheathes the sky in diffused light for many hours before a brilliant aurora. Suddenly, a swift shadow, like the fabulous flying-dragon, writhed through the air before her, and she felt herself instantly seized and borne aloft. It was that wild beast--the most savage and serpentine and subtle and fearless of our latitudes--known by hunters as the Indian Devil, and he held her in his clutches on the broad floor of a swinging fir-bough. His long sharp claws were caught in her clothing, he worried them sagaciously a little, then, finding that ineffectual to free them, he commenced licking her bare arm with his rasping tongue and pouring over her the wide streams of his hot, foetid breath. So quick had this flashing action been that the woman had had no time for alarm; moreover, she was not of the screaming kind: but now, as she felt him endeavoring to disentangle his claws, and the horrid sense of her fate smote her, and she saw instinctively the fierce plunge of those weapons, the long strips of living flesh torn from her bones, the agony, the quivering disgust, itself a worse agony,--while by her side, and holding her in his great lithe embrace, the monster crouched, his white tusks whetting and gnashing, his eyes glaring through all the darkness like balls of red fire,--a shriek, that rang in every forest hollow, that startled every winter-housed thing, that stirred and woke the least needle of the tasselled pines, tore through her lips. A moment afterward, the beast left the arm, once white, now crimson, and looked up alertly.

She did not think at this instant to call upon God. She called upon her husband. It seemed to her that she had but one friend in the world; that was he; and again the cry, loud, clear, prolonged, echoed through the woods. It was not the shriek that disturbed the creature at his relish; he was not born in the woods to be scared of an owl, you know; what then? It must have been the echo, most musical, most resonant, repeated and yet repeated, dying with long sighs of sweet sound, vibrated from rock to river and back again from depth to depth of cave and cliff. Her thought flew after it; she knew, that, even if her husband heard it, he yet could not reach her in time; she saw that while the beast listened he would not gnaw,--and this she *felt* directly, when the rough, sharp, and multiplied stings of his tongue retouched her arm. Again her lips opened by instinct, but the sound that issued thence came by reason. She had heard that music charmed wild beasts,--just this point between life and death intensified every faculty,--and when she opened her lips the third time, it was not for shrieking, but for singing.

A little thread of melody stole out, a rill of tremulous motion; it was the cradle-song with which she rocked her baby;--how could she sing that? And then she remembered the baby sleeping rosily on the long settee before the fire,--the father cleaning his gun, with one foot on the green wooden rundle,--the merry light from the chimney dancing out and through the room, on the rafters of the ceiling with their tassels of onions and herbs, on the log walls painted with lichens and festooned with apples, on the king's-arm slung across the shelf with the old pirate's-cutlass, on the snow-pile of the bed, and on the great brass clock,--dancing, too, and lingering on the baby, with his fringed-gentian eyes, his chubby fists clenched on the pillow, and his fine breezy hair fanning with the motion of his father's foot. All this struck her in one, and made a sob of her breath, and she ceased.

Immediately the long red tongue thrust forth again. Before it touched, a song sprang to her lips, a wild sea-song, such as some sailor might be singing far out on trackless blue water that night, the shrouds whistling with frost and the sheets glued in ice,--a song with the wind in its burden and the spray in its chorus. The monster raised his head and flared the fiery eyeballs upon her, then fretted the imprisoned claws a moment and was quiet; only the breath like the vapor from some hell-pit still swathed her. Her voice, at first faint and fearful, gradually lost its quaver, grew under her control and subject to her modulation; it rose on long swells, it fell in subtle cadences, now and then its tones pealed out like bells from distant belfries on fresh sonorous mornings. She sung the song through, and, wondering lest his name of Indian Devil were not his true name, and if he would not detect her, she repeated it. Once or twice now, indeed, the beast stirred uneasily, turned, and made the bough sway at his movement. As she ended, he snapped his jaws together, and tore away the fettered member, curling it under him with a snarl,--when she burst into the gayest reel that ever answered a fiddle-bow. How many a time she had heard her husband play it on the homely fiddle made by himself from birch and cherry-wood! how many a time she had seen it danced on the floor of their one room, to the patter of wooden clogs and the rustle of homespun petticoat! how many a time she had danced it herself!--and did she not remember once, as they joined clasps for eight-hands-round, how it had lent its gay, bright measure to her life? And here she was singing it alone, in the forest, at midnight, to a wild beast! As she sent her voice trilling up and down its quick oscillations between joy and pain, the creature who grasped her uncurled his paw and scratched the bark from the bough; she must vary the spell; and her voice spun leaping along the projecting points of tune of a hornpipe. Still singing, she felt herself twisted about with a low growl and a lifting of the red lip from the glittering teeth; she broke the hornpipe's thread, and commenced unravelling a lighter, livelier thing, an Irish jig. Up and down and round about her voice flew, the beast threw back his head so that the diabolical face fronted hers, and the torrent of his breath prepared her for his feast as the anaconda slimes his prey. Franticly she darted from tune to tune; his restless movements followed her. She tired herself with dancing and vivid national airs, growing feverish and singing spasmodically as she felt her horrid tomb yawning wider. Touching in this manner all the slogan and keen clan cries, the beast moved again, but only to lay the disengaged paw across her with heavy satisfaction. She did not dare to pause; through the clear cold air, the frosty starlight, she sang. If there were yet any tremor in the tone, it was not fear,--she had learned the secret of sound at last; nor could it be chill,--far too high a fever throbbed her pulses; it was nothing but the thought of the log-house and of what might be passing within it. She fancied the baby stirring in his sleep and moving his pretty lips,--her husband rising and opening the door, looking out after her, and wondering at her absence. She fancied the light pouring through the chink and then shut in again with all the safety and comfort and joy, her husband taking down the fiddle and playing lightly with his head inclined, playing while she sang, while she sang for her life to an Indian Devil. Then she knew he was fumbling for and finding some shining fragment and scoring it down the yellowing hair, and unconsciously her voice forsook the wild war-tunes and drifted into the half-gay, half-melancholy Rosin the Bow.

Suddenly she woke pierced with a pang, and the daggered tooth penetrating her flesh;--dreaming of safety, she had ceased singing and lost it. The beast had regained the use of all his limbs, and now, standing and raising his back, bristling and foaming, with sounds that would have been like hisses but for their deep and fearful sonority, he withdrew step by step toward the trunk of the tree, still with his flaming balls upon her. She was all at once free, on one end of the bough, twenty feet from the ground. She did not measure the distance, but rose to drop herself down, careless of any death, so that it were not this. Instantly, as if he scanned her thoughts, the creature bounded forward with a yell and caught her again in his dreadful hold. It might be that he was not greatly famished; for, as she suddenly flung up her voice again, he settled himself composedly on the bough, still clasping her with invincible pressure to his rough, ravenous breast, and listening in a fascination to the sad, strange U-la-lu that now moaned forth in loud, hollow tones above him. He half closed his eyes, and sleepily reopened and shut them again.

What rending pains were close at hand! Death! and what a death! worse than any other that is to be named! Water, be it cold or warm, that which buoys up blue ice-fields, or which bathes tropical coasts with currents of balmy bliss, is yet a gentle conqueror, kisses as it kills, and draws you down gently through darkening fathoms to its heart. Death at the sword is the festival of trumpet and bugle and banner, with glory ringing out around you and distant hearts thrilling through yours. No gnawing disease can bring such hideous end as this; for that is a fiend bred of your own flesh, and this--is it a fiend, this living lump of appetites? What dread comes with the thought of perishing in flames! but fire, let it leap and hiss never so hotly, is something too remote, too alien, to inspire us with such loathly horror as a wild beast; if it have a life, that life is too utterly beyond our comprehension. Fire is not half ourselves; as it devours, arouses neither hatred nor disgust; is not to be known by the strength of our lower natures let loose; does not drip our blood into our faces from foaming chaps, nor mouth nor slaver above us with vitality. Let us be ended by fire, and we are ashes, for the winds to bear, the leaves to cover; let us be ended by wild beasts, and the base, cursed thing howls with us forever through the forest. All this she felt as she charmed him, and what force it lent to her song God knows. If her voice should fail! If the damp and cold should give her any fatal hoarseness! If all the silent powers of the forest did not conspire to help her! The dark, hollow night rose indifferently over her; the wide, cold air breathed rudely past her, lifted her wet hair and blew it down again; the great boughs swung with a ponderous strength, now and then clashed their iron lengths together and shook off a sparkle of icy spears or some long-lain weight of snow from their heavy shadows. The green depths were utterly cold and silent and stern. These beautiful haunts that all the summer were hers and rejoiced to share with her their bounty, these heavens that had yielded their largess, these stems that had thrust their blossoms into her hands, all these friends of three moons ago forgot her now and knew her no longer.

Feeling her desolation, wild, melancholy, forsaken songs rose thereon from that frightful aerie,--weeping, wailing tunes, that sob among the people from age to age, and overflow with otherwise unexpressed sadness,-- all rude, mournful ballads,--old tearful strains, that

Shakespeare heard the vagrants sing, and that rise and fall like the wind and tide,--sailor-songs, to be heard only in lone mid-watches beneath the moon and stars,--ghastly rhyming romances, such as that famous one of the Lady Margaret, when

> "She slipped on her gown of green
>   A piece below the knee,--
> And 't was all a long, cold winter's night
>   A dead corse followed she."

Still the beast lay with closed eyes, yet never relaxing his grasp. Once a half-whine of enjoyment escaped him,--he fawned his fearful head upon her; once he scored her cheek with his tongue: savage caresses that hurt like wounds. How weary she was! and yet how terribly awake! How fuller and fuller of dismay grew the knowledge that she was only prolonging her anguish and playing with death! How appalling the thought that with her voice ceased her existence! Yet she could not sing forever; her throat was dry and hard; her very breath was a pain; her mouth was hotter than any desert-worn pilgrim's;--if she could but drop upon her burning tongue one atom of the ice that glittered about her!--but both of her arms were pinioned in the giant's vice. She remembered the winding-sheet, and for the first time in her life shivered with spiritual fear. Was it hers? She asked herself, as she sang, what sins she had committed, what life she had led, to find her punishment so soon and in these pangs,--and then she sought eagerly for some reason why her husband was not up and abroad to find her. He failed her,--her one sole hope in life; and without being aware of it, her voice forsook the songs of suffering and sorrow for old Covenanting hymns,--hymns with which her mother had lulled her, which the class-leader pitched in the chimney-corners,--grand and sweet Methodist hymns, brimming with melody and with all fantastic involutions of tune to suit that ecstatic worship,--hymns full of the beauty of holiness, steadfast, relying, sanctified by the salvation they had lent to those in worse extremity than hers,--for they had found themselves in the grasp of hell, while she was but in the jaws of death. Out of this strange music, peculiar to one character of faith, and than which there is none more beautiful in its degree nor owning a more potent sway of sound, her voice soared into the glorified chants of churches. What to her was death by cold or famine or wild beasts? "Though He slay me, yet will I trust in him," she sang. High and clear through the frore fair night, the level moonbeams splintering in the wood, the scarce glints of stars in the shadowy roof of branches, these sacred anthems rose,--rose as a hope from despair, as some snowy spray of flower-bells from blackest mould. Was she not in God's hands? Did not the world swing at his will? If this were in his great plan of providence, was it not best, and should she not accept it?

"He is the Lord our God; his judgments are in all the earth."

Oh, sublime faith of our fathers, where utter self-sacrifice alone was true love, the fragrance of whose unrequired subjection was pleasanter than that of golden censers swung in purple-vapored chancels!

Never ceasing in the rhythm of her thoughts, articulated in music as they thronged, the memory of her first communion flashed over her. Again she was in that distant place on that sweet spring morning. Again the congregation rustled out, and the few remained, and she trembled to find herself among them. How well she remembered the devout, quiet faces, too accustomed to the sacred feast to glow with their inner joy! how well the snowy linen at the altar, the silver vessels slowly and silently shifting! and as the cup approached and passed, how the sense of delicious perfume stole in and heightened the transport of her prayer, and she had seemed, looking up through the windows where the sky soared blue in constant freshness, to feel all heaven's balms dripping from the portals, and to scent the lilies of eternal peace! Perhaps another would not have felt so much ecstasy as satisfaction on that occasion; but it is a true, if a later disciple, who has said, "The Lord bestoweth his blessings there, where he findeth the vessels empty."

"And does it need the walls of a church to renew my communion?" she asked. "Does not every moment stand a temple four-square to God? And in that morning, with its buoyant sunlight, was I any dearer to the Heart of the World than now?-- 'My beloved is mine, and I am his," she sang over and over again, with all varied inflection and profuse tune. How gently all the winter-wrapt things bent toward her then! into what relation with her had they grown! how this common dependence was the spell of their intimacy! how at one with Nature had she become! how all the night and the silence and the forest seemed to hold its breath, and to send its soul up to God in her singing! It was no longer despondency, that singing. It was neither prayer nor petition. She had left imploring, "How long wilt thou forget me, O Lord? Lighten mine eyes, lest I sleep the sleep of death! For in death there is no remembrance of thee,"--with countless other such fragments of supplication. She cried rather, "Yea, though I walk through the valley of the shadow of death, I will fear no evil: for thou art with me; thy rod and thy staff, they comfort me,"--and lingered, and repeated, and sang again, "I shall be satisfied, when I awake, with thy likeness."

Then she thought of the Great Deliverance, when he drew her up out of many waters, and the flashing old psalm pealed forth triumphantly:--

"The lord descended from above,
        and bow'd the heavens hie:
And underneath his feet he cast
        the darknesse of the skie.
On cherubs and on cherubins
        full royally he road:
And on the wings of all the winds
        came flying all abroad."

She forgot how recently, and with what a strange
pity for her own shapeless form that was to be, she had
quaintly sung,--

"Oh, lovely appearance of death!
    What sight upon earth is so fair?
Not all the gay pageants that breathe
    Can with a dead body compare!"

She remembered instead,--"In thy presence is fulness
of joy; at thy right hand there are pleasures forevermore.
God will redeem my soul from the power of the grave:
for he shall receive me. He will swallow up death in
victory." Not once now did she say, "Lord, how long wilt
thou look on? rescue my soul from their destructions, my
darling from the lions,"--for she knew that the young
lions roar after their prey and seek their meat from God.
"O Lord, thou preservest man and beast!" she said.

She had no comfort or consolation in this season,
such as sustained the Christian martyrs in the
amphitheatre. She was not dying for her faith; there were
no palms in heaven for her to wave; but how many a
time had she declared,--"I had rather be a doorkeeper in
the house of my God, than to dwell in the tents of
wickedness!" And as the broad rays here and there broke
through the dense covert of shade and lay in rivers of
lustre on crystal sheathing and frozen fretting of trunk
and limb and on the great spaces of refraction, they
builded up visibly that house, the shining city on the hill,
and singing, "Beautiful for situation, the joy of the whole

earth, is Mount Zion, on the sides of the North, the city of the Great King," her vision climbed to that higher picture where the angel shows the dazzling thing, the holy Jerusalem descending out of heaven from God, with its splendid battlements and gates of pearls, and its foundations, the eleventh a jacinth, the twelfth an amethyst,--with its great white throne, and the rainbow round about it, in sight like unto an emerald: "And there shall be no night there,--for the Lord God giveth them light," she sang.

What whisper of dawn now rustled through the wilderness? How the night was passing! And still the beast crouched upon the bough, changing only the posture of his head, that again he might command her with those charmed eyes;--half their fire was gone; she could almost have released herself from his custody; yet, had she stirred, no one knows what malevolent instinct might have dominated anew. But of that she did not dream; long ago stripped of any expectation, she was experiencing in her divine rapture how mystically true it is that "he that dwelleth in the secret place of the Most High shall abide under the shadow of the Almighty."

Slow clarion cries now wound from the distance as the cocks caught the intelligence of day and re-echoed it faintly from farm to farm,--sleepy sentinels of night, sounding the foe's invasion, and translating that dim intuition to ringing notes of warning. Still she chanted on. A remote crash of brushwood told of some other beast on his depredations, or some night-belated traveller groping his way through the narrow path. Still she chanted on. The far, faint echoes of the chanticleers died into distance,--the crashing of the branches grew nearer. No wild beast that, but a man's step,--a man's form in the moonlight, stalwart and strong,--on one arm slept a little child, in the other hand he held his gun. Still she chanted on.

Perhaps, when her husband last looked forth, he was half ashamed to find what a fear he felt for her. He knew she would never leave the child so long but for some direst need,--and yet he may have laughed at himself, as he lifted and wrapped it with awkward care, and, loading his gun and strapping on his horn, opened the door again and closed it behind him, going out and plunging into the darkness and dangers of the forest. He was more singularly alarmed than he would have been willing to acknowledge; as he had sat with his bow hovering over the strings, he had half believed to hear her voice mingling gayly with the instrument, till he paused and listened if she were not about to lift the latch and enter. As he drew nearer the heart of the forest, that intimation of melody seemed to grow more actual, to take body and breath, to come and go on long swells and ebbs of the night-breeze, to increase with tune and words, till a strange shrill singing grew ever clearer, and, as he stepped into an open space of moonbeams, far up in the branches, rocked by the wind, and singing, "How beautiful upon the mountains are the feet of him that bringeth good tidings, that publisheth peace," he saw his wife,--his wife,--but, great God in heaven! how? Some mad exclamation escaped him, but without diverting her. The child knew the singing voice, though never heard before in that unearthly key, and turned toward it through the veiling dreams. With a celerity almost instantaneous, it lay, in the twinkling of an eye, on the ground at the father's feet, while his gun was raised to his shoulder and levelled at the monster covering his wife with shaggy form and flaming gaze,--his wife so ghastly white, so rigid, so stained with blood, her eyes so fixedly bent above, and her lips, that had indurated into the chiselled pallor of marble, parted only with that flood of solemn song.

I do not know if it were the mother-instinct that for a moment lowered her eyes,--those eyes, so lately riveted on heaven, now suddenly seeing all life-long bliss possible. A thrill of joy pierced and shivered through her like a weapon, her voice trembled in its course, her glance lost its steady strength, fever-flushes chased each other over her face, yet she never once ceased chanting. She was quite aware, that, if her husband shot now, the ball must pierce her body before reaching any vital part of the beast,--and yet better that death, by his hand, than the other. But this her husband also knew, and he remained motionless, just covering the creature with the sight. He dared not fire, lest some wound not mortal should break the spell exercised by her voice, and the beast, enraged with pain, should rend her in atoms; moreover, the light was too uncertain for his aim. So he waited. Now and then he examined his gun to see if the damp were injuring its charge, now and then he wiped the great drops from his forehead. Again the cocks crowed with the passing hour,--the last time they were heard on that night. Cheerful home sound then, how full of safety and all comfort and rest it seemed! what sweet morning incidents of sparkling fire and sunshine, of gay household bustle, shining dresser, and cooing baby, of steaming cattle in the yard, and brimming milk-pails at the door! what pleasant voices! what laughter! what security! and here--

Now, as she sang on in the slow, endless, infinite moments, the fervent vision of God's peace was gone. Just as the grave had lost its sting, she was snatched back again into the arms of earthly hope. In vain she tried to sing, "There remaineth a rest for the people of God,"-- her eyes trembled on her husband's, and she could only think of him, and of the child, and of happiness that yet might be, but with what a dreadful gulf of doubt between! She shuddered now in the suspense; all calm forsook her; she was tortured with dissolving heats or frozen with icy blasts; her face contracted, growing small and pinched; her voice was hoarse and sharp,--every tone cut like a knife,--the notes became heavy to lift,-- withheld by some hostile pressure,--impossible. One gasp, a convulsive effort, and there was silence,--she had lost her voice.

The beast made a sluggish movement,--stretched and fawned like one awakening,--then, as if he would have yet more of the enchantment, stirred her slightly with his muzzle. As he did so, a sidelong hint of the man standing below with the raised gun smote him; he sprung round furiously, and, seizing his prey, was about to leap into some unknown airy den of the topmost branches now waving to the slow dawn. The late moon had rounded through the sky so that her gleam at last fell full upon the bough with fairy frosting; the wintry morning light did not yet penetrate the gloom. The woman, suspended in mid-air an instant, cast only one agonized glance beneath,--but across and through it, ere the lids could fall, shot a withering sheet of flame,--a rifle-crack, half-heard, was lost in the terrible yell of desperation that bounded after it and filled her ears with savage echoes, and in the wide arc of some eternal descent she was falling;--but the beast fell under her.

I think that the moment following must have been too sacred for us, and perhaps the three have no special interest again till they issue from the shadows of the wilderness upon the white hills that skirt their home. The father carries the child hushed again into slumber, the mother follows with no such feeble step as might be anticipated. It is not time for reaction,--the tension not yet relaxed, the nerves still vibrant, she seems to herself like some one newly made; the night was a dream; the present stamped upon her in deep satisfaction, neither weighed nor compared with the past; if she has the careful tricks of former habit, it is as an automaton; and as they slowly climb the steep under the clear gray vault and the paling morning star, and as she stops to gather a spray of the red-rose berries or a feathery tuft of dead grasses for the chimney-piece of the log-house, or a handful of brown cones for the child's play,--of these quiet, happy folk you would scarcely dream how lately they had stolen from under the banner and encampment of the great King Death. The husband proceeds a step or two in advance; the wife lingers over a singular foot-print in the snow, stoops and examines it, then looks up with a hurried word. Her husband stands alone on the hill, his arms folded across the babe, his gun fallen,--stands defined as a silhouette against the pallid sky. What is there in their home, lying below and yellowing in the light, to fix him with such a stare? She springs to his side. There is no home there. The log-house, the barns, the neighboring farms, the fences, are all blotted out and mingled in one smoking ruin. Desolation and death were indeed there, and beneficence and life in the forest. Tomahawk and scalping-knife, descending during that night, had left behind them only this work of their accomplished hatred and one subtle foot-print in the snow.

For the rest,--the world was all before them, where to choose.

IN A CELLAR

IT WAS THE DAY of Madame de St. Cyr's dinner, an event I never missed; for, the mistress of a mansion in the Faubourg St. Germain, there still lingered about her the exquisite grace and good-breeding peculiar to the old regime, that insensibly communicates itself to the guests till they move in an atmosphere of ease that constitutes the charm of home. One was always sure of meeting desirable and well-assorted people here, and a contre-temps was impossible. Moreover, the house was not at the command of all; and Madame de St. Cyr, with the daring strength which, when found in a woman at all, should, to be endurable, be combined with a sweet but firm restraint, rode rough-shod over the parvenus of the Empire, and was resolute enough to insulate herself even among the old noblesse, who, as all the world knows, insulate themselves from the rest of France. There were rare qualities in this woman, and were I to have selected one who with an even hand should carry a snuffy candle through a magazine of powder, my choice would have devolved upon her; and she would have done it.

I often looked, and not unsuccessfully, to discern what heritage her daughter had in these little affairs. Indeed, to one like myself, Delphine presented the worthier study. She wanted the airy charm of manner, the suavity and tenderness of her mother, — a deficiency easily to be pardoned in one of such delicate and extraordinary beauty. And perhaps her face was the truest index of her mind; not that it ever transparently displayed a genuine emotion, — Delphine was too well bred for that, — but the outline of her features had a keen regular precision, as if cut in a gem. Her exquisite color seldom varied, her eyes were like blue steel, she was statuelike and stony. But had one paused there, pronouncing her hard and impassive, he had committed an error. She had no great capability for passion, but she was not to be deceived; one metallic flash of her eye would cut like a sword through the whole mesh of entanglements with which you had surrounded her; and frequently, when alone with her, you perceived cool recesses in her nature, sparkling and pleasant, which jealously guarded themselves from a nearer approach. She was infinitely spirituelle; compared to her, Madame herself was heavy.

At the first, I had seen that Delphine must be the wife of a diplomate. What diplomate? For a time asking myself the question seriously, I decided in the negative, which did not, however, prevent Delphine from fulfilling her destiny, since there were others. She was, after all, like a draught of rich old wine, all fire and sweetness. These things were not generally seen in her; I was more favored than many; and I looked at her with pitiless perspicacious eyes. Nevertheless, I had not the least advantage; it was, in fact, between us, diamond cut diamond, — which, oddly enough, brings me back to my story.

Some years previously, I had been sent on a special mission to the government at Paris, and having finally executed it, I resigned the post, and resolved to make my residence there, since it is the only place on earth where one can live. Every morning I half expect to see the country, beyond the city, white with an encampment of the nations, who, having peacefully flocked there over night, wait till the Rue St. Honoré shall run out and greet them. It surprises me, sometimes, that those pretending to civilization are content to remain at a distance. What experience have they of life, — not to mention gayety and pleasure, but of the great purpose of life, — society? Man evidently is gregarious; Fourier's fables are founded on fact; we are nothing without our opposites, our fellows, our lights and shadows, colors, relations, combinations, our point d'appui, and our angle of sight. An isolated man is immensurable; he is also unpicturesque, unnatural, untrue. He is no longer the lord of Nature, animal and vegetable, — but Nature is the lord of him; the trees, skies, flowers, predominate, and he is in as bad taste as green and blue, or as an oyster in a vase of roses. The race swings naturally to clusters. It being admitted, then, that society is our normal state, where is it to be obtained in such perfection as at Paris? Show me the urbanity, the generosity in trifles, better than sacrifice, the incuriousness and freedom, the grace, and wit, and honor, that will equal such as I find here. Morality, — we were not speaking of it, — the intrusion is unnecessary; must that word with Anglo-Saxon pertinacity dog us round the world? A hollow mask, which Vice now and then lifts for a breath of air, I grant you this state may be called; but since I find the vice elsewhere, countenance my preference for the accompanying mask. But even this is vanishing; such drawing-rooms as Mme. de St. Cyr's are less and less frequent. Yet, though the delightful spell of the last century daily dissipates itself, and we are not now what we were twenty years ago, still Paris is, and will be to the end of time, for a cosmopolitan, the pivot on which the world revolves.

It was, then, as I have said, the day of Mme. de St. Cyr's dinner. Punctually at the hour, I presented myself, — for I have always esteemed it the least courtesy which a guest can render, that he should not cool his hostess's dinner.

The usual choice company waited. There was the Marquis of G., the ambassador from home; Col. Leigh, an attaché of that embassy; the Spanish and Belgian ministers; — all of whom, with myself, completed a diplomatic circle. There were also wits and artists, but no ladies whose beauty exceeded that of the St. Cyrs. With nearly all of this assemblage I held certain relations, so that I was immediately at ease. G. was the only one whom, perhaps, I would rather not have met, although we were the best of friends. They awaited but one, the Baron Stahl. Meanwhile Delphine stood coolly taking the measurement of the Marquis of G., while her mother entertained one and another guest with a low-toned flattery, gentle interest, or lively narration, as the case might demand.

In a country where a coup d'état was as easily given as a box on the ear, we all attentively watched for the arrival of one who had been sent from a neighboring empire to negotiate a loan for the tottering throne of this. Nor was expectation kept long on guard. In a moment, "His Excellency, the Baron Stahl!" was announced.

The exaggeration of his low bow to Mme. de St. Cyr, the gleam askance of his black eye, the absurd simplicity of his dress, did not particularly please me. A low forehead, straight black brows, a beardless cheek with a fine color which give him a fictitiously youthful appearance, were the most striking traits of his face; his person was not to be found fault with; but he boldly evinced his admiration for Delphine, and with a wicked eye.

As we were introduced, he assured me, in pure English, that he had pleasure in making the acquaintance of a gentleman whose services were so distinguished.

I, in turn, assured him of my pleasure in meeting a gentleman who appreciated them.

I had arrived at the house of Mme. de St. Cyr with a load on my mind, which for four weeks had weighed there; but before I thus spoke, it was lifted and gone. I had seen the Baron Stahl before, although not previously aware of it; and now, as he bowed, talked my native tongue so smoothly, drew a glove over the handsome hand upon whose first finger shone the only incongruity of his attire, a broad gold ring, holding a gaudy red stone, — as he stood smiling and expectant before me, a sudden chain of events flashed through my mind, an instantaneous heat, like lightning, welded them into logic. A great problem was resolved. For a second, the breath seemed snatched from my lips; the next, a lighter, freer man never trod in diplomatic shoes.

I really beg your pardon, — but perhaps from long usage, it has become impossible for me to tell a straight story. It is absolutely necessary to inform you of events already transpired.

In the first place, then, I, at this time, possessed a valet, the pink of valets, an Englishman, — and not the less valuable to me in a foreign capital, that, notwithstanding his long residence, he was utterly unable to speak one word of French intelligibly. Reading and writing it readily, his thick tongue could master scarcely a syllable. The adroitness and perfection with which he performed the duties of his place were unsurpassable. To a certain extent I was obliged to admit him into my confidence; I was not at all in his. In dexterity and despatch he equalled the advertisements. He never condescended to don my cast-off apparel, but, disposing of it, always arrayed himself in plain but gentlemanly garments. These do not complete the list of Hay's capabilities. He speculated. Respectable tenements in London called him landlord; in the funds certain sums lay subject to his order; to a profitable farm in Hants he contemplated future retirement; and passing upon the Bourse, I have received a grave bow, and have left him in conversation with an eminent capitalist respecting consols, drafts, exchange, and other erudite mysteries, where I yet find myself in the A B C. Thus not only was my valet a free-born Briton, but a landed proprietor. If the Rothschilds blacked your boots or shaved your chin, your emotions might be akin to mine. When this man, who had an interest in the India traders, brought the hot water into my dressing-room, of a morning, the Antipodes were tributary to me. To what extent might any little irascibility of mine drive a depression in the market! and I knew, as he brushed my hat, whether stocks rose or fell. In one respect, I was essentially like our Saxon ancestors, — my servant was a villain. If I had been merely a civilian, in any purely private capacity, having leisure to attend to personal concerns in the midst of the delicate specialties intrusted to me from the cabinet at home, the possession of so inestimable a valet might have bullied me beyond endurance. As it was, I found it rather agreeable than otherwise. He was tacitly my secretary of finance.

Several years ago, a diamond of wonderful size and beauty, having wandered from the East, fell into certain imperial coffers among our Continental neighbors; and at the same time some extraordinary intelligence, essential to the existence, so to speak, of that government, reached a person there who fixed as its price this diamond. After a while he obtained it, but, judging that prudence lay in departure, took it to England, where it was purchased for an enormous sum by the Duke of — as he will remain an unknown quantity, let us say X.

There are probably not a dozen such diamonds in the world, — certainly not three in England. It rejoiced in such flowery appellatives as the Sea of Splendor, the Moon of Milk; and, of course, those who had but parted with it under protest, as it were, determined to obtain it again at all hazards; — they were never famous for scrupulosity The Duke of X. was aware of this, and, for a time, the gem had lain idle, its glory muffled in a casket; but finally, on some grand occasion a few months prior to the period of which I have spoken above, it was determined to set it in the Duchess's coronet. Accordingly, one day, it was given by her son, the Marquis of G., into the hands of their solicitor, who should deliver it to her Grace's jeweller. It lay in a small shagreen case, and before the Marquis left, the solicitor placed the case in a flat leathern box, where lay a chain of most singular workmanship, the clasp of which was deranged. This chain was very broad, of a style known as the brickwork, but every brick was a tiny gem, set in a delicate filagree linked with the next, and the whole rainbowed lustrousness moving at your will, like the scales of some gorgeous Egyptian serpent; — the solicitor was to take this also to the jeweller. Having laid the box in his private desk, Ulster, his confidential clerk, locked it, while he bowed the Marquis down. Returning immediately, the solicitor took the flat box and drove to the jeweller's. He found the latter so crowded with customers, it being the fashionable hour, as to be unable to attend to him; he, however, took the solicitor into his inner room, a dark fire-proof place, and there quickly deposited the box within a safe, which stood inside another, like a Japanese puzzle, and the solicitor, seeing the doors double-locked and secured, departed; the other promising to attend to the matter on the morrow.

Early the next morning, the jeweller entered his dark room, and proceeded to unlock the safe. This being concluded, and the inner one also thrown open, he found the box in a last and entirely, as he had always believed, secret compartment. Anxious to see this wonder, this Eye of Morning, and Heart of Day, he eagerly loosened the band and unclosed the box. It was empty. There was no chain there; the diamond was missing. The sweat streamed from his forehead, his clothes were saturated, he believed himself the victim of a delusion. Calling an assistant, every article and nook in the dark room was examined. At last, in an extremity of despair, he sent for the solicitor, who arrived in a breath. The jeweller's alarm hardly equalled that of the other. In his sudden dismay, he at first forgot the circumstances and dates relating to the affair; afterward was doubtful. The Marquis of G. was summoned, the police called in, the jeweller given into custody. Every breath the solicitor continued to draw only built up his ruin. He swallowed laudanum, but, by making it an overdose, frustrated his own design. He was assured, on his recovery, that no suspicion attached to him. The jeweller now asseverated that the diamond had never been given to him; but though the jeweller had committed perjury, this was, nevertheless, strictly true. Of course, whoever had the stone would not attempt to dispose of it at present, and, though communications were opened with the general

European police, there was very little to work upon. But by means of this last step the former possessors became aware of its loss, and I make no doubt had their agents abroad immediately.

Meanwhile, the case hung here, complicated and tantalizing, when one morning I woke in London. No sooner had G. heard of my arrival than he called, and, relating the affair, requested my assistance. I confess myself to have been interested, — foolishly so, I thought afterward; but we all have our weaknesses, and diamonds were mine. In company with the Marquis, I waited upon the solicitor, who entered into the few details minutely, calling frequently upon Ulster, a young, fresh-looking man, for corroboration. We then drove to the jeweller's new quarters, took him, under charge of the officers, to his place of business, where he nervously showed me every point that could bear upon the subject, and ended by exclaiming, that he was ruined, and all for a stone he had never seen. I sat quietly for a few moments. It stood, then, thus: — G. had given the thing to the solicitor, seen it put into the box, seen the box put into the desk; but while the confidential clerk, Ulster, locked the desk, the solicitor waited on the Marquis to the door, — returning, took the box, without opening it again, to the jeweller, who, in the hurry, shut it up in his safe, also without opening it. The case was perfectly clear. These mysterious things are always so simple! You know now as well as I, who took the diamond.

I did not choose to volunteer, but assented, on being desired. The police and I were old friends; they had so often assisted me, that I was not afraid to pay them in kind, and accordingly agreed to take charge of the case, still retaining their aid, should I require it. The jeweller was now restored to his occupation, although still subjected to a rigid surveillance, and I instituted inquiries into the recent movements of the young man Ulster. The case seemed to me to have been very blindly conducted. But, though all that was brought to light concerning him in London was perfectly fair and aboveboard, it was discovered that, not long since, he had visited Paris, — on the solicitor's business, of course, but gaining thereby an opportunity to transact any little affairs of his own. This was fortunate; for if any one could do anything in Paris, it was myself.

It is not often that I act as a detective. But one homogeneous to every situation could hardly play a pleasanter part for once. I have thought that our great masters in theory and practice, Machiavel and Talleyrand, were hardly more, on a large scale.

I was about to return to Paris, but resolved to call previously on the solicitor again. He welcomed me warmly, although my suspicions had not been imparted to him, and, with a more cheerful heart than had lately been habitual to him, entered into an animated conversation respecting the great case of Biter v. Bit, then absorbing so much of the public attention, frequently addressing Ulster, whose remarks were always pertinent, brief, and clear. As I sat actively discussing the topic, feeling no more interest in it than in the end of that cigar I just cut off, and noting exactly every look and motion of the unfortunate youth, I recollect the curious sentiment that filled me regarding him. What injury had he done me, that I should pursue him with punishment? Me? I am, and every individual is, integral with the commonwealth. It was the commonwealth he had injured. Yet, even then, why was I the one to administer justice? Why not continue with my coffee in the morning, my kings and cabinets and national chess at noon, my opera at night, and let the poor devil go? Why, but that justice is brought home to every member of society, — that naked duty requires no shirking of such responsibility, — that, had I failed here, the crime might, with reason, lie at my door and multiply, the criminal increase himself?

Very possibly you will not unite with me; but these little catechisms are, once in a while, indispensable, to vindicate one's course to one's self.

This Ulster was a handsome youth; — the rogues have generally all the good looks. There was nothing else remarkable about him but his quickness; he was perpetually on the alert; by constant activity, the rust was never allowed to collect on his faculties; his sharpness was distressing, — he appeared subject to a tense strain. Now his quill scratched over the paper unconcernedly, while he could join as easily in his master's conversation: nothing seemed to preoccupy him, or he held a mind open at every point. It is pitiful to remember him that morning, sitting quiet, unconscious, and free, utterly in the hands of that mighty Inquisition, the Metropolitan Police, with its countless arms, its cells and myrmidons in the remotest corners of the Continent, — at the mercy of so merciless a monster, and momently closer involved, like some poor prey round which a spider spins its bewildering web. It was also curious to observe the sudden suspicion that darkened his face at some innocent remark, — the quick shrinking and intrenched retirement, the manifest sting and rancor, as I touched his wound with a swift flash of my slender weapon and sheathed it again, and, after the thrust, the espionage, and the relief at believing it accidental. He had many threads to gather up and hold; — little electric warnings along them must have been constantly shocking him. He did that part well enough; it was a mistake, to begin with; he needed prudence. At that time I owed this Ulster nothing; now, however, I owe him a grudge, for some of the most harassing hours of my life were occasioned me by him. But I shall not cherish enmity on that account. With so promising a beginning, he will graduate and take his degree from the loftiest altitude in his line. Hemp is a narcotic; let it bring me forgetfulness.

In Paris I found it not difficult to trace such a person, since he was both foreign and unaccustomed. It was ascertained that he had posted several letters. A person of his description had been seen to drop a letter, the superscription of which had been read by one who picked it up for him. This superscription was the address of the very person who was likely to be the agent of the former possessors of the diamond, and had attracted attention. After all, — you know the Secret Force, — it was not so impossible to imagine what this letter contained, despite of its cipher. Such a person also had been met among the Jews, and at certain shops whose reputation was not of the clearest. He had called once or twice on Mme. de St. Cyr, on business relative to a vineyard adjoining her chateau in the Gironde, which she had sold to a wine merchant of England. I found a zest in the affair, as I pursued it.

We were now fairly at sea, but before long I found we were likely to remain there; in fact, nothing of consequence eventuated. I began to regret having taken the affair from the hands in which I had found it, and one day, it being a gala or some insatiable saint's day, I was riding, perplexed with that and other matters, and paying small attention to the passing crowd. I was vexed and mortified, and had fully decided to throw up the whole, — on such hairs do things hang, — when, suddenly turning a corner, my bridle-reins became entangled in the snaffle of another rider. I loosened them abstractedly, and not till it was necessary to bow to my strange antagonist on parting, did I glance up. The person before me was evidently not accustomed to play the dandy; he wore his clothes ill, sat his horse worse, and was uneasy in the saddle. The unmistakable air of the gamin was apparent beneath the superficies of the gentleman. Conspicuous on his costume, and wound like an order of merit upon his breast, glittered a chain, the chain, — each tiny brick-like gem spiked with a hundred sparks, and building a fabric of sturdy probabilities with the celerity of the genii in constructing Aladdin's palace. There, a cable to haul up the treasure, was the chain; — where was the diamond? I need not tell you how I followed this young friend, with what assiduity I kept him in sight, up and down, all day long, till, weary at last of his fine sport, as I certainly was of mine, he left his steed in stall and fared on his way a-foot. Still pursuing, now I threaded quay and square, street and alley, till he disappeared in a small shop, in one of those dark crowded lanes leading eastward from the Pont Neuf, in the city. It was the sign of a marchand des armures, and having provided myself with those persuasive arguments, a sergent-de-ville and a gendarme, I entered.

A place more characteristic it would be impossible to find. Here were piled bows of every material, ash, and horn, and tougher fibres, with slackened strings, and among them peered a rusty clarion and battle-axe, while the quivers that should have accompanied lay in a distant corner, their arrows serving to pin long, dusty, torn banners to the wall. Opposite the entrance, an archer in bronze hung on tiptoe, and levelled a steel bow, whose piercing fleche seemed sparkling with impatience to spring from his finger and flesh itself in the heart of the intruder. The hauberk and halberd, lance and casque, arquebuse and sword, were suspended in friendly congeries; and fragments of costly stuff swept from ceiling to floor, crushed and soiled by the heaps of rusty firelocks, cutlasses, and gauntlets thrown upon them. In one place, a little antique bust was half hid in the folds of some pennon, still dyed with battle-stains; in another, scattered treasures of Dresden and Sevres brought the drawing-room into the campaign; and all around bivouacked rifles, whose polished barrels glittered full of death, — pistols, variously mounted, for an insurgent at the barricades, or for a lost millionnaire at the gaming-table, — foils, with buttoned bluntness, — and rapiers whose even edges were viewless as if filed into air. Destruction lay everywhere, at the command of the owner of this place, and, had he possessed a particle of vivacity, it would have been hazardous to bow beneath his doorway. It did not, I must say, look like a place where I should find a diamond. As the owner came forward, I determined on my plan of action.

"You have, sir," I said, handing him a bit of paper, on which were scrawled some numbers, "a diamond in your possession, of such and so many carats, size, and value, belonging to the Duke of X., and left with you by an Englishman, Mr. Arthur Ulster. You will deliver it to me, if you please."

"Monsieur!" exclaimed the man, lifting his hands, and surveying me with the widest eyes I ever saw. "A diamond! In my possession! So immense a thing! It is impossible. I have not even seen one of the kind. It is a mistake. Jacques Noailles, the vender of jewels en gros, second door below, must be the man. One should perceive that my business is with arms, not diamonds. I have it not; it would ruin me."

Here he paused for a reply, but, meeting none, resumed. "M. Arthur Ulster! — I have heard of no such person. I never spoke with an Englishman. Bah! I detest them! I have no dealings with them. I repeat, I have not your jewel. Do you wish anything more of me?"

His vehemence only convinced me of the truth of my suspicions.

"These heroics are out of place," I answered. "I demand the article in question."

"Monsieur doubts me?" he asked, with a rueful face, — "questions my word, which is incontrovertible?" Here he clapped his hand upon a couteau-de-chasse lying near, but, appearing to think better of it, drew himself up, and, with a shower of nods flung at me, added, "I deny your accusation!" I had not accused him.

"You are at too much pains to convict yourself. I charge you with nothing," I said. "But this diamond must be surrendered."

"Monsieur is mad!" he exclaimed, "mad! he dreams! Do I look like one who possesses such a trophy? Does my shop resemble a mine? Look about! See! All that is here would not bring a hundredth part of its price. I beseech Monsieur to believe me; he has mistaken the number, or has been misinformed."

"We waste words. I know this diamond is here, as well as a costly chain — "

"On my soul, on my life, on my honor," he cried clasping his hands and turning up his eyes, "there is here nothing of the kind. I do not deal in gems. A little silk, a few weapons, a curiosity, a nicknack, comprise my stock. I have not the diamond. I do not know the thing. I am poor. I am honest. Suspicion destroys me!"

"As you will find, should I be longer troubled by your denials."

He was inflexible, and, having exhausted every artifice of innocence, wiped the tears from his eyes, — oh, these French! life is their theatre, — and remained quiet. It was getting dark. There was no gas in the place; but in the pause a distant street-lamp swung its light dimly round.

"Unless one desires to purchase, allow me to say that it is my hour for closing," he remarked, blandly, rubbing his black-bearded chin.

"My time is valuable," I returned. "It is late and dark. When your shop-boy lights up — "

"Pardon, — we do not light."

"Permit me, then, to perform that office for you. In this blaze you may perceive my companions, whom you have not appeared to recognize."

So saying, I scratched a match upon the floor, and, as the sergent-de-ville and the gendarme advanced, threw the light of the blue spirit of sulphurous flame upon them. In a moment more the match went out, and we remained in the demi-twilight of the distant lantern. The marchand des armures stood petrified and aghast. Had he seen the imps of Satan in that instant, it could have had no greater effect.

"You have seen them?" I asked. "I regret to inconvenience you; but unless this diamond is produced at once, my friends will put their seal on your goods, your property will be confiscated, yourself in a dungeon. In other words, I allow you five minutes; at the close of that time you will have chosen between restitution and ruin."

He remained apparently lost in thought. He was a big, stout man, and with one blow his powerful fist could easily have settled me. It was the last thing in his mind. At length he lifted his head, — "Rosalie!" he called.

At the word, a light foot pattered along a stone floor within, and in a moment a little woman stood in an arch raised by two steps from our own level. Carrying a candle, she descended and tripped toward him. She was not pretty, but sprightly and keen, as the perpetual attrition of life must needs make her, and wore the everlasting grisette costume, which displays the neatest of ankles, and whose cap is more becoming than wreaths of garden millinery. I am too minute, I see, but it is second nature. The two commenced a vigorous whispering amid sundry gestures and glances. Suddenly the woman turned, and, laying the prettiest of little hands on my sleeve, said, with a winning smile, —

"Is it a crime of lèse-majesté?"

This was a new idea, but might be useful.

"Not yet," I said; "two minutes more, and I will not answer for the consequence.'

Other whispers ensued.

"Monsieur," said the man, leaning on one arm over the counter, and looking up in my face, with the most engaging frankness, — "it is true that I have such a diamond; but it is not mine. It is left with me to be delivered to the Baron Stahl, who comes as an agent from his court for its purchase."

"Yes, — I know."

"He was to have paid me half a million francs, — not half its worth, — in trust for the person who left it, who is not M. Arthur Ulster, but Mme. de St. Cyr."

Madame de St. Cyr! How under the sun — No, — it could not be possible. The case stood as it stood before. The rogue was in deeper water than I had thought; he had merely employed Mme. de St. Cyr. I ran this over in my mind, while I said, "Yes."

"Now, sir," I continued, "you will state the terms of this transaction."

"With pleasure. For my trouble I was myself to receive patronage and five thousand francs. The Baron is to be here directly, on other and public business. Reine du ciel, Monsieur! how shall I meet him?"

"He is powerless in Paris; your fear is idle."

"True. There were no other terms."

"Nor papers?"

"The lady thought it safest to be without them. She took merely my receipt, which the Baron Stahl will bring to me from her before receiving this."

"I will trouble you for it now."

He bowed and shuffled away. At a glance from me, the gendarme slipped to the rear of the building, where three others were stationed at the two exits in that direction, to caution them of the critical moment, and returned. Ten minutes passed, — the merchant did not appear. If, after all, he had made off with it! There had been the click of a bolt, the half-stifled rattle of arms, as if a door had been opened and rapidly closed again, but nothing more.

"I will see what detains my friend," said Mademoiselle, the little woman.

We suffered her to withdraw. In a moment more a quick expostulation was to be heard.

"They are there, the gendarmes, my little one! I should have run, but they caught me, the villains! and replaced me in the house. Oh, sacre!" — and rolling this word between his teeth, he came down and laid a little box on the counter. I opened it. There was within a large, glittering, curiously cut piece of glass. I threw it aside.

"The diamond!" I exclaimed.

"Monsieur had it," he replied, stooping to pick up the glass with every appearance of surprise and care.

"Do you mean to say you endeavored to escape with that bawble? Produce the diamond instantly, or you shall hang as high as Haman!" I roared.

Whether he knew the individual in question or not, the threat was efficient; he trembled and hesitated, and finally drew the identical shagreen case from his bosom.

"I but jested," he said. "Monsieur will witness that I relinquish it with reluctance."

"I will witness that you receive stolen goods!" I cried, in wrath.

He placed it in my hands.

"Oh!" he groaned, from the bottom of his heart, hanging his head, and laying both hands on the counter before him, — "it pains, it grieves me to part with it!"

"And the chain," I said.

"Monsieur did not demand that!"

"I demand it now."

In a moment, the chain also was given me.

"And now will Monsieur do me a favor? Will he inform me by what means he ascertained these facts?"

I glanced at the garcon, who had probably supplied himself with his masters finery illicitly; — he was the means; — we have some generosity; — I thought I should prefer doing him the favor, and declined.

I unclasped the shagreen case; the sergent-de-ville and the gendarme stole up and looked over my shoulder; the garcon drew near with round eyes; the little woman peeped across; the merchant, with tears streaming over his face, gazed as if it had been a loadstone; finally, I looked myself. There it lay, the glowing, resplendent thing! flashing in affluence of splendor, throbbing and palpitant with life, drawing all the light from the little woman's candle, from the sparkling armor around, from the steel barbs, and the distant lantern, into its bosom. It was scarcely so large as I had expected to see it, but more brilliant than anything I could conceive of. I do not believe there is another such in the world. One saw clearly that the Oriental superstition of the sex of stones was no fable; this was essentially the female of diamonds, the queen herself, the principle of life, the rejoicing receptive force. It was not radiant, as the term literally taken implies; it seemed rather to retain its wealth, — instead of emitting its glorious rays, to curl them back like the fringe of a madrepore, and lie there with redoubled quivering scintillations, a mass of white magnificence, not prismatic, but a vast milky lustre. I closed the case; on reopening it, I could scarcely believe that the beautiful sleepless eye would again flash upon me. I did not comprehend how it could afford such perpetual richness, such sheets of lustre.

At last we compelled ourselves to be satisfied. I left the shop, dismissed my attendants, and, fresh from the contemplation of this miracle, again trod the dirty, reeking streets, crossed the bridge, with its lights, its warehouses midway, its living torrents who poured on unconscious of the beauty within their reach. The thought of their ignorance of the treasure, not a dozen yards distant, has often made me question if we all are not equally unaware of other and greater processes of life, of more perfect, sublimed and, as it were, spiritual crystallizations going on invisibly about us. But had these been told of the thing clutched in the hand of a passer, how many of them would have know where to turn? and we, — are we any better?

II

FOR a few days I carried the diamond about my person, and did not mention its recovery even to my valet, who knew that I sought it, but communicated only with the Marquis of G., who replied, that he would be in Paris on a certain day, when I could safely deliver it to him.

It was now generally rumored that the neighboring government was about to send us the Baron Stahl, ambassador concerning arrangements for a loan to maintain the sinking monarchy in supremacy at Paris, the usual synecdoche for France.

The weather being fine, I proceeded to call on Mme. de St. Cyr. She received me in her boudoir, and on my way thither I could not but observe the perfect quiet and cloistered seclusion that prevaded the whole house, — the house itself seeming only an adjunct of the still and sunny garden, of which one caught a glimpse through the long open hall- windows beyond. This boudoir did not differ from others to which I have been admitted: the same delicate shades; all the dainty appliances of Art for beauty; the lavish profusion of bijouterie; and the usual statuettes of innocence, to indicate, perhaps, the presence of that commodity which might not be guessed at otherwise; and burning in a silver cup, a rich perfume loaded the air with voluptuous sweetness. Through a half-open door an inner boudoir was to be seen, which must have been Delphine's; it

looked like her; the prevailing hue was a soft purple, or
gray; a prie-dieu, a bookshelf, and desk, of a dark West
Indian wood, were just visible. There was but one
picture, — a sad-eyed, beautiful Fate. It was the type of
her nation. I think she worshipped it. And how apt is
misfortune to degenerate into Fate! — not that the girl
had ever experienced the former, but, dissatisfied with
life, and seeing no outlet, she accepted it stoically and
waited till it should be over. She needed to be aroused;
— the station of an ambassadrice, which I desired for
her, might kindle the spark. There were no flowers, no
perfumes, no busts, in this ascetic place. Delphine
herself, in some faint rosy gauze, her fair hair streaming
round her, as she lay on a white-draped couch, half-risen
on one arm, while she read the morning's feuilleton, was
the most perfect statuary of which a room could boast,
— illumined, as I saw her, by the gay beams that entered
at the loftily-arched window, broken only by the
flickering of the vine-leaves that clustered the curiously-
latticed panes without. She resembled in kind a Nymph,
just bursting from the sea; so Pallas might have posed for
Aphrodite. Madame de St. Cyr received me with
empressement, and, so doing, closed the door of this
shrine. We spoke of various things, — of the court, the
theatre, the weather, the world, — skating lightly round
the slender edges of her secret, till finally she invited me
to lunch with her in the garden. Here, on a rustic table,
stood wine and a few delicacies, — while, by extending a
hand, we could grasp the hanging pears and nectarines,
still warm to the lip and luscious with sunshine, as we

disputed possession with the envious wasp who had established a priority of claim.

"It is to be hoped," I said, sipping the Haut-Brion, whose fine and brittle smack contrasted rarely with the delicious juiciness of the fruit, "that you have laid in a supply of this treasure that neither moth nor rust doth corrupt, before parting with that little gem in the Gironde."

"Ah? You know, then, that I have sold it?"

"Yes," I replied. "I have the pleasure of Mr. Ulster's acquaintance."

"He arranged the terms for me," she said, with restraint, — adding, "I could almost wish now that it had not been."

This was probably true; for the sum which she hoped to receive from Ulster for standing sponsor to his jewel was possibly equal to the price of her vineyard.

"It was indispensable at the time, this sale; I thought best to hazard it on one more season. — If, after such advantages, Delphine will not marry, why — it remains to retire into the country and end our days with the barbarians!" she continued, shrugging her shoulders; "I have a house there."

"But you will not be obliged to throw us all into despair by such a step now," I replied.

She looked quickly, as if to see how nearly I had approached her citadel, — then, finding in my face no expression but a complimentary one, "No," she said, "I hope that my affairs have brightened a little. One never knows what is in store."

Before long I had assured myself that Mme. de St. Cyr was not a party to the theft, but had merely been hired by Ulster, who, discovering the state of her affairs, had not, therefore, revealed his own, — and this without in the least implying any knowledge on my part of the transaction. Ulster must have seen the necessity of leaving the business in the hands of a competent person, and Mme. de St. Cyr's financial talent was patent. There were few ladies in Paris who would have rejected the opportunity. Of these things I felt a tolerable certainty.

"We throng with foreigners," said Madame, archly, as I reached this point. "Diplomates, too. The Baron Stahl arrives in a day."

"I have heard," I responded. "You are acquainted?"

"Alas! no," she said. "I knew his father well, though he himself is not young. Indeed, the families thought once of intermarriage. But nothing has been said on the subject for many years. His Excellency, I hear, will strengthen himself at home by an alliance with the young Countess, the natural daughter of the Emperor."

"He surely will never be so imprudent as to rivet his chain by such a link!"

"It is impossible to compute the dice in those despotic countries," she rejoined, — which was pretty well, considering the freedom enjoyed by France at that period.

"It may be," I suggested, "that the Baron hopes to open this delicate subject with you yourself, Madame."

"It is unlikely," she said, sighing. "And for Delphine, should I tell her his excellency preferred scarlet, she would infallibly wear blue. Imagine her, Monsieur, in fine scarlet, with a scarf of gold gauze, and rustling grasses in that unruly gold hair of hers! She would be divine!"

The maternal instinct as we have it here at Paris confounds me. I do not comprehend it. Here was a mother who did not particularly love her child, who would not be inconsolable at her loss, would not ruin her own complexion by care of her during illness, would send her through fire and water and every torture to secure or maintain a desirable rank, who yet would entangle herself deeply in intrigue, would not hesitate to tarnish her own reputation, and would, in fact, raise heaven and earth to — endow this child with a brilliant match. And Mme. de St. Cyr seemed to regard Delphine, still further, as a cool matter of Art.

These little confidences, moreover, are provoking. They put you yourself so entirely out of the question.

"Mlle. de St. Cyr's beauty is peerless," I said, slightly chagrined, and at a loss. "If hearts were trumps, instead of diamonds!"

"We are poor," resumed Madame, pathetically. "Delphine is not an heiress. Delphine is proud. She will not stoop to charm. Her coquetry is that of an Amazon. Her kisses are arrows. She is Medusa!" And Madame, her mother, shivered.

Here, with her hair knotted up and secured by a tiny dagger, her gauzy drapery gathered in her arm, Delphine floated down the green alley toward us, as if in a rosy cloud. But this soft aspect never could have been more widely contradicted than by the stony repose and cutting calm of her beautiful face.

"The Marquis of G.," said her mother, "he also arrives ambassador. Has he talent? Is he brilliant? Wealthy, of course, — but gauche?"

Therewith I sketched for them the Marquis and his surroundings.

"It is charming," said Madame. "Delphine, do you attend?"

"And why?" asked Delphine, half concealing a yawn with her dazzling hand. "It is wearisome; it matters not to me."

"But he will not go to marry himself in France," said her mother. "Oh, these English," she added, with a laugh, "yourself, Monsieur, being proof of it, will not mingle blood, lest the Channel should still flow between the little red globules! You will go? but to return shortly? You will dine with me soon? Au revoir!" and she gave me her hand graciously, while Delphine bowed as if I were already gone, threw herself into a garden-chair, and commenced pouring the wine on a stone for a little tame snake which came out and lapped it.

Such women as Mme. de St. Cyr have a species of magnetism about them. It is difficult to retain one's self-respect before them, — for no other reason than that one is, at the moment, absorbed into their individuality, and thinks and acts with them. Delphine must have had a strong will, and perpetual antagonism did not weaken it. As for me, Madame had, doubtless, reasons of her own for tearing aside these customary bands of reserve — reasons which, if you do not perceive, I shall not enumerate.

III

"HAVE YOU MET WITH anything further in your search, sir?" asked my valet next morning.

"Oh, yes, Hay," I returned, in a very good humor, — "with great success. You have assisted me so much, that I am sure I owe it to you to say that I have found the diamond."

"Indeed, sir, you are very kind. I have been interested, but my assistance is not worth mentioning. I thought likely it might be, you appeared so quiet." — The cunning dog! — "How did you find it, sir, may I ask?"

I briefly related the leading facts, since he had been aware of the progress of the case to that point, — without, however, mentioning Mme. de St. Cyr's name.

"And Monsieur did not inform us!" a French valet would have cried.

"You were prudent not to mention it, sir," said Hay. "These walls must have better ears than ordinary; for a family has moved in on the first floor recently, whose actions are extremely suspicious. But is this precious affair to be seen?"

I took it from an inner pocket and displayed it, having discarded the shagreen case as inconvenient.

"His Excellency must return as he came," said I.

Hay's eyes sparkled.

"And do you carry it there, sir?" he asked, with surprise, as I restored it to my waistcoat-pocket.

"I shall take it to the bank," I said. "I do not like the responsibility."

"It is very unsafe," was the warning of this cautious fellow. "Why, sir! any of these swells, these pickpockets, might meet you, run against you, — so!" said Hay, suiting the action to the word," and, with the little sharp knife concealed in just such a ring as this I wear, give a light tap, and there's a slit in your vest sir, but no diamond!" — and instantly resuming his former respectful deportment, Hay handed me my gloves and stick, and smoothed my hat.

"Nonsense!" I replied, drawing on the gloves, "I should like to see the man who could be too quick for me. Any news from India, Hay?"

"None of consequence, sir. The indigo crop is said to have failed which advances the figure of that on hand, so that one or two fortunes will be made to-day. Your hat, sir? — your lunettes? Here they are, sir."

"Good morning, Hay."

"Good morning, sir."

I descended the stairs, buttoning my gloves, paused a moment at the door to look about, and proceeded down the street, which was not more than usually thronged. At the bank I paused to assure myself that the diamond was safe. My fingers caught in a singular slit. I started. As Hay had prophesied there was a fine longitudinal cut in my waistcoat, but the pocket was empty. My God! the thing was gone. I never can forget the blank nihility of all existence that dreadful moment when I stood fumbling for what was not. Calm as I sit here and tell of it, I vow to you a shiver courses through me at the very thought. I had circumvented Stahl only to destroy myself. The diamond was lost again. My mind flew like lightning over every chance, and a thousand started up like steel spikes to snatch the bolt. For a moment I was stunned, but, never being very subject to despair, on my recovery, which was almost at once, took every measure that could be devised. Who had touched me? Whom had I met? Through what streets had I come? In ten minutes the Prefect had the matter in hand. My injunctions were strict privacy. I sincerely hoped the mishap would not reach England; and if the diamond were not recovered before the Marquis of G. arrived, — why, there was the Seine. It is all very well to talk, — yet suicide is so French an affair, that an Englishman does not take to it naturally, and, except in November, the Seine is too cold and damp for comfort, but during that month I suppose it does not greatly differ in these respects from our own atmosphere.

A preternatural activity now possessed me. I slept none, ate little, worked immoderately. I spared no efforts, for everything was at stake. In the midst of all, G. arrived. Hay also exerted himself to the utmost; I promised him a hundred pounds, if I found it. He never told me that he said how it would be, never intruded the state of the market, never resented my irritating conduct, but watched me with narrow yet kind solicitude, and frequently offered valuable suggestions, which, however, as everything else did, led to nothing. I did not call on G., but in a week or so his card was brought up one morning to me. "Deny me," I groaned. It yet wanted a week of the day on which I had promised to deliver him the diamond Meanwhile the Baron Stahl had reached Paris, but he still remained in private, — few had seen him.

The police were forever on the wrong track. Today they stopped the old Comptesse du Quesne and her jewels, at the Barriere; to-morrow, with their long needles, they riddled a package of lace destined for the Duchess of X. herself; the Secret Service was doubled; and to crown all, a splendid new star of the testy Prince de Ligne was examined and proclaimed to be paste, — the Prince swearing vengeance, if he could discover the cause, — while half Paris must have been under arrest. My own hotel was ransacked thoroughly, — Hay begging that his traps might be included, — but nothing resulted, and I expected nothing, for, of course, I could swear that the stone was in my pocket when I stepped into the street. I confess I never was nearer madness, — every word and gesture stung me like asps, — I walked on burning coals. Enduring all this torment, I must yet meet my daily comrades, eat ices at Tortoni's, stroll on the Boulevards, call on my acquaintance, with the same equanimity as before. I believe I was equal to it. Only by contrast with that blessed time when Ulster and diamonds were unknown, could I imagine my past happiness, my present wretchedness. Rather than suffer it again, I would be stretched on the rack till ever! bone in my skin were broken. I cursed Mr. Arthur Ulster every hour in the day; myself, as well; and even now the word diamond sends a cold blast to my heart. I often met my friend the marchand des armures. It was his turn to triumph; I fancied there must be a hang-dog kind of air about me, as about every sharp man who has been outwitted. It wanted finally but two days of that on which I was to deliver the diamond.

One midnight, armed with a dark lantern and a cloak, I was traversing the streets alone, — unsuccessful, as usual, just now solitary, and almost in despair. As I turned a corner, two men were but scarcely visible a step before me. It was a badly-lighted part of the town. Unseen and noiseless I followed. They spoke in low tones, — almost whispers; or rather, one spoke, — the other seemed to nod assent.

"On the day but one after to-morrow," I heard spoken in English. Great Heavens! was it possible? had I arrived at a clew? That was the day of days for me. "You have given it, you say, in this billet, — I wish to be exact, you see," continued the voice, — "to prevent detection, you gave it, ten minutes after it came into your hands, to the butler of Madame ," (here the speaker stumbled on the rough pavement, and I lost the name,) "who," he continued, "will put it in the —" (a second stumble acted like a hiccough) "cellar."

"Wine-cellar," I thought; "and what then?"

"In the ——." A third stumble was followed by a round German oath. How easy it is for me now to fill up the little blanks which that unhappy pavement caused!

"You share your receipts with this butler. On the day I obtain it," he added, and I now perceived his foreign accent, "I hand you one hundred thousand francs; afterward, monthly payments till you have received the stipulated sum. But how will this butler know me, in season to prevent a mistake? Hem! — he might give it to the other!"

My hearing had been trained to such a degree that I would have promised to catch any given dialogue of the spirits themselves, but the whisper that answered him eluded me. I caught nothing but a faint sibillation. "Your ring?" was the rejoinder. "He shall be instructed to recognize it? Very well. It is too large, — no, that will do, it fits the first finger. There is nothing more. I am under infinite obligations, sir; they shall be remembered. Adieu!"

The two parted; which should I pursue? In desperation I turned my lantern upon one, and illumined a face fresh with color, whose black eyes sparkled askance after the retreating figure, under straight black brows. In a moment more he was lost in a false cul-de-sac, and I found it impossible to trace the other.

I was scarcely better off than before; but it seemed to me that I had obtained something, and that now it was wisest to work this vein. "The butler of Madame — —." There were hundreds of thousands of Madames in town. I might call on all, and he as old as the Wandering Jew at the last call. The cellar. Wine-cellar, of course, — that came by a natural connection with butler, — but whose? There was one under my own abode; certainly I would explore it. Meanwhile, let us see the entertainments for Wednesday. The Prefect had a list of these. For some I found I had cards; I determined to allot a fraction of time to as many as possible; my friends in the Secret Service would divide the labor. Among others, Madame de St. Cyr gave a dinner, and, as she had been in the affair, I determined not to neglect her on this occasion, although having no definite idea of what had been, or plan of what should be done. I decided not to speak of this occurrence to Hay, since it might only bring him off some trail that he had struck.

Having been provided with keys, early on the following evening I entered the wine-cellar, and, concealed in an empty cask that would have held a dozen of me, waited for something to turn up. Really, when I think of myself, a diplomate, a courtier, a man-about-town, curled in a dusty, musty wine-barrel, I am moved with vexation and laughter. Nothing, however, turned up, — and at length I retired baffled. The next night came, — no news, no identification of my black-browed man, no success; but I felt certain that something must transpire in that cellar. I don't know why I had pitched upon that one in particular, but, at an earlier hour than on the previous night, I again donned the cask. A long time must have elapsed; dead silence filled the spacious vaults, except where now and then some Sillery cracked the air with a quick explosion, or some newer wine bubbled round the bung of its barrel with a faint effervescence. I had no intention of leaving this place till morning, but it suddenly appeared like the most woeful waste of time. The master of this tremendous affair should be abroad and active; who knew what his keen eyes might detect; what loss his absence might occasion in this nick of time? And here he was, shut up and locked in a wine-cellar! I began to be very nervous; I had already, with aid, searched every crevice of the cellar; and now I thought it would be some consolation to discover the thief, if I never regained the diamond. A distant clock tolled midnight. There was a faint noise, — a mouse? — no, it was too prolonged; — nor did it sound like the fiz of Champagne; — a great iron door was turning on its hinges; a man with a lantern was entering; another followed, and another. They seated themselves. In a few moments, appearing one by one and at intervals, some thirty people were in the cellar. Were they all to share in the proceeds of the diamond? With what jaundiced eye we behold things! I myself saw all that was only through the lens of this diamond, of which not one of these men had ever heard. As the lantern threw its feeble glimmer on this group, and I surveyed them through my loophole, I thought I had never seen so wild and savage a picture, such enormous shadows, such bold outline, such a startling flash on the face of their leader, such light retreating up the threatening arches. More resolute brows, more determined words, more unshrinking hearts, I had not met. In fact, I found myself in the centre of a conspiracy, a society as vindictive as the Jacobins, as unknown and terrible as the Marianne of to-day. I was thunderstruck, too, at the countenances on which the light fell, — men the loyalest in estimation, ministers and senators, millionnaires who had no reason for discontent, dandies whose reason was supposed to be devoted to their tailors, poets and artists of generous aspiration and suspected tendencies, and one woman, — Delphine de St. Cyr. Their plans were brave, their determination lofty, their conclave serious and fine; yet as slowly they shut up their hopes and fears in the black masks, one man bent toward the lantern to adjust his. When he lifted his face before concealing it, I recognized him also. I had met him frequently at the Bureau of Police; he was, I believe, Secretary of the Secret Service.

I had no sympathy with these people. I had sufficient liberty myself, I was well enough satisfied with the world, I did not care to revolutionize France; but my heart rebelled at the mockery, as this traitor and spy, this creature of a system by which I gained my fame, showed his revolting face and veiled it again. And Delphine, what had she to do with them? One by one, as they entered, they withdrew, and I was left alone again. But all this was not my diamond.

Another hour elapsed. Again the door opened, and remained ajar. Some one entered, whom I could not see. There was a pause, — then a rustle, — the door creaked ever so little. "Art thou there?" lisped a shrill whisper, — a woman, as I could guess.

"My angel, it is I," was returned, a semitone lower. She approached, he advanced, and the consequence was a salute resonant as the smack with which a Dutch burggomaster may be supposed to set down his mug. I was prepared for anything. Ye gods! if it should be Delphine! But the base suspicion was birth-strangled as they spoke again. The conversation which now ensued between these lovers under difficulties was tender and affecting beyond expression. I had felt guilty enough when an unwilling auditor of the conspirators, — since, though one employs spies, one does not therefore act that part one's self, but on emergencies, — an unwillingness which would not, however, prevent my turning to advantage the information gained; but here, to listen to this rehearsal of woes and blisses, this ah mon Fernand, this aria in an area, growing momently more fervent, was too much I overturned the cask, scrambled upon my feet, and fled from the cellar leaving the astounded lovers to follow, while, agreeably to my instincts and regardless of the diamond, I escaped the embarrassing predicament.

At length it grew to be noon of the appointed day. Nothing had transpired; all our labor was idle. I felt, nevertheless, more buoyant than usual, — whether because I was now to put my fate to the test, or that today was the one of which my black-browed man had spoken, and I therefore entertained a presentiment of good fortune, I cannot say. But when, in unexceptionable toilet, I stood on Mme. de St. Cyr's steps, my heart sunk. G. was doubtless already within, and I thought of the marchand des armures' exclamation, "Queen of Heaven, Monsieur! how shall I meet him!" I was plunged at once into the profoundest gloom. Why had I undertaken the business at all? This interference, this good-humor, this readiness to oblige, — it would ruin me yet! I forswore it, as Falstaff forswore honor. Why needed I to meddle in the melee? Why — But I was no catechumen. Questions were useless now. My emotions are not chronicled on my face, I flatter myself; and with my usual repose I saluted our hostess. Greeting G. without any allusion to the diamond, the absence of which allusion he received as a point of etiquette, I was conversing with Mrs. Leigh, when the Baron Stahl was announced. I turned to look at his Excellency. A glance electrified me. There was my dark-browed man of the midnight streets. It must, then, have been concerning the diamond that I had heard him speak. His countenance, his eager glittering eye, told that to-day was as eventful to him as to me. If he were here, I could well afford to be. As he addressed me in English, my certainty was confirmed; and the instant in which I observed the ring, gaudy and coarse, upon his finger, made confirmation doubly sure. I own I was surprised that anything could induce the Baron to wear such an ornament. Here he was actually risking his reputation as a man of taste, as an exquisite, a leader of haut ton, a gentleman, by the detestable vulgarity of this ring. But why do I speak so of the trinket? Do I not owe it a thrill of as fine joy as I ever knew? Faith! it was not unfamiliar to me. It had been a daily sight for years. In meeting the Baron Stahl I had found the diamond.

The Baron Stahl was then, the thief? Not at all. My valet, as of course you have been all along aware, was the thief.

My valet, moreover, was my instructor; he taught me not again to scour Cathay for what might be lying under my hand at home. Nor have I since been so acute as to overreach myself. Yet I can explain such intolerable stupidity only by remembering that when one has been in the habit of pointing his telescope at the stars, he is not apt to turn it upon pebbles at his feet.

The Marquis of G. took down Mme. de St. Cyr; Stahl preceded me, with Delphine. As we sat at table, G. was at the right, I at the left of our hostess Next G. sat Delphine; below her, the Baron; so that we were nearly vis-à-vis. I was now as fully convinced that Mme. de St. Cyr's cellar was the one, as the day before I had been that the other was; I longed to reach it. Hay had given the stone to a butler — doubtless this — the moment of its theft; but, not being aware of Mme. de St. Cyr's previous share in the adventure, had probably not afforded her another. And thus I concluded her to be ignorant of the game we were about to play; and I imagined, with the interest that one carries into a romance, the little preliminary scene between the Baron and Madame that must have already taken place, being charmed by the cheerfulness with which she endured the loss of the promised reward.

As the Baron entered the dining-room, I saw him withdraw his glove, and move the jewelled hand across his hair while passing the solemn butler, who gave it a quick recognition; — the next moment we were seated. There were only wines on the table, clustered around a central ornament, — a bunch of tall silver rushes and flagleaves, on whose airy tip danced fleurs-de-lis of frosted silver, a design of Delphine's, — the dishes being on sidetables, from which the guests were served as they signified their choice of the variety on their cards. Our number not being large, and the custom so informal, rendered it pleasant.

I had just finished my oysters and was pouring out a glass of Chablis, when another plate was set before the Baron.

"His Excellency has no salt," murmured the butler, — at the same time placing one beside him. A glance, at entrance, had taught me that most of the service was uniform; this dainty little saliere I had noticed on the buffet, solitary, and unlike the others. What a fool had I been! Those gaps in the Baron's remarks caused by the pavingstones, how easily were they to be supplied!

"Madame?"

Madame de St. Cyr.

"The cellar?"

A salt-cellar.

How quick the flash that enlightened me while I surveyed the saliere!

"It is exquisite! Am I never to sit at your table but some new device charms me?" I exclaimed. "Is it your design, Mademoiselle?" I said, turning to Delphine.

Delphine, who had been ice to all the Baron's advances, only curled her lip. "Des babioles!" she said.

"Yes, indeed!" cried Mme. de St. Cyr, extending her hand for it. "But none the less her taste. Is it not a fairy thing? À Cellini! Observe this curve, these lines! but one man could have drawn them!" — and she held it for our scrutiny. It was a tiny hand and arm of ivory, parting the foam of a wave and holding a golden shell, in which the salt seemed to have crusted itself as if in some secretest ocean-hollow. I looked at the Baron a moment; his eyes were fastened upon the saliere, and all the color had forsaken his cheeks, — his face counted his years. The diamond was in that little shell. But how to obtain it? I had no novice to deal with; nothing but finesse would answer.

"Permit me to examine it?" I said. She passed it to her left hand for me to take. The butler made a step forward.

"Meanwhile, Madame," said the Baron, smiling, "I have no salt."

The instinct of hospitality prevailed; — she was about to return it. Might I do an awkward thing? Unhesitatingly. Reversing my glass, I gave my arm a wider sweep than necessary, and, as it met her hand with violence, the saliere fell. Before it touched the floor I caught it. There was still a pinch of salt left, — nothing more.

"A thousand pardons!" I said, and restored it to the Baron.

His Excellency beheld it with dismay; it was rare to see him bend over and scrutinize it with starting eyes.

"Do you find there what Count Arnaldos begs in the song," asked Delphine, — "the secret of the sea, Monsieur?"

He handed it to the butler, observing, "I find here no — "

"Salt, Monsieur?" replied the man, who did not doubt but all had gone right, and replenished it.

Had one told me in the morning, that no intricate manœuvres, but a simple blunder, would effect this, I might have met him in the Bois de Boulogne.

"We will not quarrel," said my neighbor, lightly, with reference to the popular superstition

"Rather propitiate the offended deities by a crumb tossed over the shoulder," added I.

"Over the left?" asked the Baron, to intimate his knowledge of another idiom, together with a reproof for my gauchene.

"A gauche, — quelquefois c'est justement a droit, " I replied.

"Salt in any pottage," said Madame, a little uneasily, "is like surprise in an individual; it brings out the flavor of every ingredient, so my cook tells me."

"It is a preventive of palsy," I remarked, as the slight trembling of my adversary's finger caught my eye.

"And I have noticed that a taste for it is peculiar to those who trace their blood," continued Madame.

"Let us, therefore, elect a deputation to those mines near Cracow," said Delphine.

"To our cousins, the slaves there?" laughed her mother.

"I must vote to lay your bill on the table, Mademoiselle," I rejoined.

"But with a boule blanche, Monsieur?"

"As the salt has been laid on the floor," said the Baron.

Meanwhile, as this light skirmishing proceeded, my sleeve and Mme. de St. Cyr's dress were slightly powdered, but I had not seen the diamond. The Baron, bolder than I, looked under the table, but made no discovery. I was on the point of dropping my napkin to accomplish a similar movement when my accommodating neighbor dropped hers. To restore it, I stooped. There it lay, large and glowing, the Sea of Splendor, the Moon of Milk, the Torment of my Life, on the carpet, within half an inch of a lady's slipper Mademoiselle de St. Cyr's foot had prevented the Baron from seeing it; now it moved and unconsciously covered it. All was as I wished. I hastily restored the napkin, and looked steadily at Delphine, — so steadily, that she perceived some meaning, as she had already suspected a game. By my sign she understood me, pressed her foot upon the stone and drew it nearer. In France we do not remain at table until unfit for a lady's society, — we rise with them. Delphine needed to drop neither napkin nor handkerchief; she composedly stooped and picked up the stone, so quickly at no one saw what it was.

"And the diamond?" said the Baron to the butler, rapidly, as he passed.

"It was in the saliere," whispered the astonished creature.

IV

IN THE DRAWING-ROOM I sought the Marquis.

"To-day I was to surrender you your property," I said; "it is here."

"Do you know," he replied, "I thought I must have been mistaken?"

"Any of our volatile friends here might have been," I resumed; "for us it is impossible. Concerning this, when you return to France, I will relate the incidents; at present, there are those who will not hesitate to take life to obtain its possession. A conveyance leaves in twenty minutes; and if I owned the diamond, it should not leave me behind. Moreover, who knows what a day may bring forth? To-morrow there may be an émeute. Let me restore the thing as you withdraw."

The Marquis, who is not, after all, the Lion of England, pausing a moment to transmit my words from his ear to his brain, did not afterward delay to make inquiries or adieux, but went to seek Mme. de St. Cyr and wish her good-night, on his departure from Paris. As I awaited his return, which I knew would not be immediate, Delphine left the Baron and joined me.

"You beckoned me?" she asked.

"No, I did not."

"Nevertheless, I come by your desire, I am sure."

"Mademoiselle," I said, "I am not in the custom of doing favors; I have forsworn them. But before you return me my jewel, I risk my head and render one last one, and to you."

"Do not, Monsieur, at such price," she responded, with a slight mocking motion of her hand.

"Delphine! those resolves, last night, in the cellar, were daring, the were noble, yet they were useless."

She had not started, but a slight tremor ran over her person and vanished while I spoke.

"They will be allowed to proceed no farther, — the axe is sharpened; for the last man who adjusted his mask was a spy, — was the Secretary of the Secret Service

Delphine could not have grown paler than was usual with her of late. She flashed her eye upon me.

"He was, it may be, Monsieur himself," she said.

"I do not claim the honor of that post."

"But you were there, nevertheless, — a spy!"

"Hush, Delphine! It would be absurd to quarrel. I was there for the recovery of this stone, having heard that it was in a cellar, — when, stupidly enough, I had insisted should be a wine-cellar."

"It was, then — "

"In a salt-cellar, — a blunder which, as you do not speak English, you cannot comprehend. I never mix with treason, and did not wish to assist at your pastimes. I speak now, that you may escape."

"If Monsieur betrays his friends, the police, why should I expect a kinder fate?"

"When I use the police, they are my servants, not my friends. I simply warn you, that, before sunrise, you will be safer travelling than sleeping, — safer next week in Vienna than in Paris."

"Thank you! And the intelligence is the price of the diamond? If I had not chanced to pick it up, my throat," and she clasped it with her fingers, "had been no slenderer than the others?"

"Delphine, will you remember, should you have occasion to do so in Vienna, that it is just possible for an Englishman to have affections, and sentiments, and, in fact, sensations? that, with him, friendship can be inviolate, and to betray it an impossibility? And even were it not, I, Mademoiselle have not the pleasure to be classed by you as a friend."

"You err. I esteem Monsieur highly."

I was impressed by her coolness.

"Let me see if you comprehend the matter," I demanded.

"Perfectly. The arrest will be used to-night, the guillotine tomorrow."

"You will take immediate measures for flight?"

"No, — I do not see that life has value. I shall be the debtor of him who takes it."

"A large debt. Delphine, I exact a promise of you. I do not care to have endangered myself for nothing. It is not ù worth while to make your mother unhappy. Life is not yours to throw away. I appeal to your magnanimity."

"'Affections, sentiments, sensations!'" she quoted. "Your own danger for the affection, — it is an affair of the heart! Mme. de St. Cyr's unhappiness, — there is the sentiment. You are angry, Monsieur, — that must be the sensation."

"Delphine, I am waiting."

"Ah, well. You have mentioned Vienna, — and why? Liberals are countenanced there?"

"Not in the least. But Madame l'Ambassadrice will be countenanced.'

"I do not know her."

"We are not apt to know ourselves."

"Monsieur, how idle are these cross-purposes!" she said, folding her fan.

"Delphine," I continued, taking the fan, "tell me frankly which of these two men you prefer, — the Marquis or his Excellency."

"The Marquis? He is antiphlogistic, — he is ice. Why should I freeze myself? I am frozen now, — I need fire!"

Her eyes burned as she spoke, and a faint red flushed her cheek.

"Mademoiselle, you demonstrate to me that life has yet a value to you."

"I find no fire," she said, as the flush fell away.

"The Baron?"

"I do not affect him."

"You will conquer your prejudice in Vienna."

"I do not comprehend you, Monsieur; — you speak in riddles, which I do not like."

"I will speak plainer. But first let me ask you for the diamond."

"The diamond? It is yours? How am I certified of it? I find it on the floor; you say it was in my mother's saliere; it is her affair, not mine. No, Monsieur, I do not see that the thing is yours."

Certainly there was nothing to be done but to relate the story, which I did, carefully omitting the Baron's name. At its conclusion, she placed the prize in my hand.

"Pardon, Monsieur." she said; "without doubt you should receive it. And this agent of the government, — one could turn him like hot iron in this vice, — who was he?"

"The Baron Stahl."

All this time G. had been waiting on thorns, and, leaving her now, I approached him, displayed for an instant the treasure on my palm, and slipped it into his. It was done. I bade farewell to this Eye of Morning and Heart of Day, this thing that had caused me such pain and perplexity and pleasure, with less envy and more joy than I thought myself capable of. The relief and buoyancy that seized me, as his hand closed upon it, I shall not attempt to portray. An abdicated king was not freer.

The Marquis departed, and I, wandering round the salon, was next stranded upon the Baron. He was yet hardly sure of himself. We talked indifferently for a few moments, and then I ventured on the great loan. He was, as became him, not communicative, but scarcely thought it would be arranged. I then spoke of Delphine.

"She is superb!" said the Baron, staring at her boldly.

She stood opposite, and, in her white attire on the background of the blue curtain, appeared like an impersonation of Greek genius relieved upon the blue of an Athenian heaven. Her severe and classic outline, her pallor, her downcast lids, her absorbed look, only heightened the resemblance. Her reverie seemed to end abruptly, the same red stained her cheek again, her lips curved in a proud smile, she raised her glowing eyes and observed us regarding her. At too great distance to hear our words, she quietly repaid our glances in the strength of her new decision, and then, turning, began to entertain those next her with an unwonted spirit.

"She has needed," I replied to the Baron, "but one thing, — to be aroused, to be kindled. See, it is done! I have thought that a life of cabinets and policy might achieve this, for her talent is second not even to her beauty."

"It is unhappy that both should be wasted," said the Baron. "She, of course, will never marry."

"Why not?"

"For various reasons."

"One?"

"She is poor."

"Which will not signify to your Excellency. Another?"

"She is too beautiful. One would fall in love with her. And to love one's own wife — it is ridiculous!"

"Who should know?" I asked.

"All the world would suspect and laugh."

"Let those laugh that win."

"No, — she would never do as a wife; but then as ____"

"But then in France we do not insult hospitality!"

The Baron transferred his gaze to me for a moment, then tapped his snuff-box, and approached the circle round Delphine.

It was odd that we, the arch enemies of the hour, could speak without the intervention of seconds; but I hoped that the Baron's conversation might be diverting, — the Baron hoped that mine might be didactic.

They were very gay with Delphine. He leaned on the back of a chair and listened. One spoke of the new gallery of the Tuileries, and the five pavilions, — a remark which led us to architecture.

"We all build our own houses," said Delphine, at last, "and then complain that they cramp us here, and the wind blows in there, while the fault is not in the order, but in us, who increase here and shrink there without reason."

"You speak in metaphors," said the Baron.

"Precisely. A truth is often more visible veiled than nude."

"We should soon exhaust the orders," I interposed; "for who builds like his neighbor?"

"Slight variations, Monsieur! Though we take such pains to conceal the style, it is not difficult to tell the order of architecture chosen by the builders in this room. My mother, for instance — you perceive that her pavilion would be the florid Gothic."

"Mademoiselle's is the Doric," I said.

"Has been," she murmured, with a quick glance.

"And mine, Mademoiselle?" asked the Baron, indifferently.

"Ah, Monsieur," she returned, looking serenely upon him, "when one has all the winning cards in hand and yet loses the stake, we allot him un pavillon chinois." — which was the polite way of dubbing him Court Fool.

The Baron's eyes fell. Vexation and alarm were visible on his contracted brow. He stood in meditation for some time. It must have been evident to him that Delphine knew of the recent occurrences, — that here in Paris she could denounce him as the agent of a felony, the participant of a theft. What might prevent it? Plainly but one thing: no woman would denounce her husband. He had scarcely contemplated this step on arrival.

The guests were again scattered in groups round the room. I examined an engraving on an adjacent table. Delphine reclined as lazily in a fauteuil as if her life did not hang in the balance. The Baron drew near.

"Mademoiselle," said he, "you allotted me just now a cap and bells. If two should wear it? — if I should invite another into my pavillon chinois? — if I should propose to complete an alliance, desired by my father, with the ancient family of St. Cyr? — if, in short, Mademoiselle, I should request you to become my wife?"

"Eh, bien, Monsieur, — and if you should?" I heard her coolly reply.

But it was no longer any business of mine. I rose and sought Mme. de St. Cyr, who, I thought, was slightly uneasy, perceiving some mystery to be afloat. After a few words, I retired.

Archimedes, as perhaps you have never heard, needed only a lever to move the world. Such a lever I had put into the hands of Delphine, with which she might move, not indeed the grand globe, with its multiplied attractions, relations, and affinities, but the lesser world of circumstances, of friends and enemies, the circle of hopes, fears, ambitions. There is no woman, as I believe, but could have used it.

V

THE NEXT DAY was scarcely so quiet in the city as usual. The great loan had not been negotiated. Both the Baron Stahl and the English minister had left Paris, — and there was a coup d'état.

But the Baron did not travel alone. There had been a ceremony at midnight in the Church of St. Sulpice, and her excellency the Baroness Stahl, nee de St. Cyr, accompanied him.

It is a good many years since. I have seen the diamond in the Duchess of X.'s coronet, once, when a young queen put on her royalty, — but I have never seen Delphine. The Marquis begged me to retain the chain, and I gave myself the pleasure of presenting it, through her mother, to the Baroness Stahl. I hear, that, whenever she desires to effect any cherished object which the Baron opposes, she has only to wear this chain, and effect it. It appears to possess a magical power, and its potent spell enslaves the Baron as the lamp and ring of Eastern tales enslaved the Afrites. The life she leads has aroused her. She is no longer the impassive Silence; she has found her fire. I hear of her as the charm of a brilliant court, as the soul of a nation of intrigue. Of her beauty one does not speak, but her talent is called prodigious. What impels me to ask the idle question, If it were well to save her life for this? Undoubtedly she fills a station which, in that empire, must be the summit of a woman's ambition. Delphine's Liberty was not a principle, but a dissatisfaction. The Baroness Stahl is vehement, is Imperialist, is successful. While she lives, it is on the top of the wave; when she dies — ah! what business has Death in such a world?

As I said, I have never seen Delphine since her marriage. The beautiful statuesque girl occupies a niche into which the blazing and magnificent intrigante cannot crowd. I do not wish to be disillusioned. She has read me a riddle, — Delphine is my Sphinx.

VI

AS FOR MR. HAY — I once said the Antipodes were tributary to me, not thinking that I should ever become tributary to the Antipodes. But such is the case; since, partly through my instrumentality, that enterprising individual has been located in their vicinity, where diamonds are not to be had for the asking, and the greatest rogue is not a Baron.

THE MAD LADY

CERTAINLY there was a house there, half-way up Great Hill, a mansion of pale cream-colored stone, built with pillared porch and wings, vines growing over some parts of it, a sward like velvet surrounding it; the sun was flashing back from the windows--but--Why? Why had none of the Godsdale people seen that house before? Could the work of building have gone on sheltered by the thick wood in front, the laborers and the materials coming up the other side of the hill? It would not be visible now if, overnight, vistas had not been cut in the wood.

The Godsdale people seldom climbed the hill; there were rumors of ill- doing there in long past days, there were perhaps rattlesnakes, it was difficult except from the other side, there was nothing to see when you arrived, and few ever wandered that way. Why any one should wish to build there was a mystery. As the villagers stared at the place they saw, or thought they saw, swarthy turbaned servitors moving about, but so far off as to be indistinct. In fact, it was all very indistinct; so much so that Parson Solewise even declared there was no house there at all. But when Mr. Dunceby, the schoolmaster, opened his spy-glass and saw a lady--who, he said, was tall, was dark, was beautiful, with flowing draperies about her of black and filmy stuff-- come down the terrace-steps and enter a waiting automobile that speedily passed round the scarp of the hill and went down the other side, the thing was proved. Mr. Ditton, the village lawyer, also saw it without having recourse to the spy-glass; but as Mr. Ditton had but lately had what he called a nip, and indeed several of them, he was in that happy state of sweet good nature which agrees with the last speaker.

Every day for several days, even weeks, the lady was seen to enter the automobile, and be taken round the side of the hill and down to the plain intersected by many roads and ending in a marsh bounded by the great river. The car would go some distance, and then, apparently at an order given through the long speaking-tube, would turn about and take a different course, only to be as quickly reversed and sent to another road on the right or on the left. Sometimes it would seem to certain of the adventurous youth coming and going on the great plain that the chauffeur remonstrated, but evidently the more she insisted, and the car went on swiftly in the new direction, wrecklessly plunging and rocking over deep-rutted places as if both driver and passenger were mad. Indeed they came to call the woman the Mad Lady. She seemed to be on a wild search for something that lay she knew not where, or for the right road to it in all the tangle of roads. One day, it was Mr. Dunceby and Mr. Ditton who, coming from a fishing-trip--Mr. Ditton's flask quite empty--saw a ride which they averred was the wildest piece of daredeviltry ever known, or would have been but for the black tragedy at its end.

The car was speeding down Springwood way, as if running a race with the wind, when suddenly it swerved, backed, and turned about, going diagonally opposite into

Blueberry lane, crossed over from that by a short cut to Commoners, only to reverse again--the lady inside, as well as they could see, giving contradictory and excited orders--and after one or two more turns and returns and zigzags, the car shot forward with incredible swiftness, as if the right way were found at last, straight down the long dike or causeway over which the farmers hauled their salt hay from the marsh in winter--the marsh now swollen to a morass by the high tides and recent rains. And then, as if in the accelerating speed the chauffeur found himself helpless, they saw the car bound into the air--at least Mr. Ditton did--the lady fling the door open, crying: "It is here! It is here!" pitching forward at the words and tossed out like a leaf, the chauffeur thrown off as violently, and all plunged into the morass, sucked down by the quicksand, and seen no more.

When a deputation of the Godsdale people, the constable, the parson, the schoolmaster, Mr. Ditton, and some others, climbed the path to Great Hill top, they found the house there quite empty, no living soul to be seen, and without furnishing of any kind. Was it possible that every one had absconded during the time in which the people had exclaimed and discussed and delayed, and that they had taken rugs and hangings and paintings and statuary with them? Or, as Parson Solewise conjectured, had there never been anything of the sort there? Yet there were others who, on returning to the village, vowed that the rich rugs, the soft draperies, the wonderful pictures they had seen were something not known by them to exist before, and that turbaned slaves were packing them away with celerity.

One thing certainly was strange: a wing of the house had vanished, the porch and the eastern wing were there, but there was no west wing; if there ever had been the grass was growing over it. The schoolmaster said it was due to the perspective; they would see it when down in the village again. And so they did. Mr. Ditton, however, went back to review the case; but, on the spot again, there was no western wing to that strange building.

The automobile was raised by some friendly hands, chiefly boys, cleansed, and taken up Great Hill and left in its place. After that, for some years the good people of Godsdale talked of the mansion, and marvelled, and borrowed the schoolmaster's spy-glass to look at it. But at last it was as an old story, and half forgotten at that; and then one and another had died; and no one came to claim the place; and other things filled the mind.

It so chanced that Mary Solewise, the old parson's daughter, one afternoon in her rambles with her lover, came out on the half- forgotten house and, stepping across the terrace, looked in at one of the windows that at a little distance had seemed to stare at them. Her lover was the young poet who had come to Godsdale for the sake of its quiet, that he might finish his epic to the resonance of no other noise than the tune in his thought. The epic is quite unknown now; but we all know and sing his songs, which are pieces of perfection. But he himself said Mary Solewise was the best poem he had found.

With a little money, some talent, and plenty of time, he was content till this song of Mary began to sing in his heart; and then when he found she was his for this life and all life to come, he found also that his small income needed to be trebled; it was too narrow a mantle to stretch over himself and Mary too. He could, after a fashion, make the little money sufficient, perhaps his verses would bring in something--verse had made more poets than Tennyson rich--but there was no roof to shelter her. And so in the midst of his happiness he was wretched. He could not enjoy the sunshine for fear of a weather- breeder. Of course if he chose to go back, if he chose to submit--but that sacrifice of honor was not to be dreamed. He lived in the hope that his epic would bring immediate fame and fortune, but, alas, his life and thought were so taken up by Mary that he could not work on the epic at all. They went off and sat down on the edge of the terrace. The great house, in the flickering afternoon sunshine through the shadows of leaves, seemed to tremble. One felt it might melt away. There was to the poet something really appealing about it. "This forsaken place has a personality," he said. "It seems as if it were asking some one to come and companion it, to save it from itself and the doom of forsaken things."

It was very evidently, indeed, by way of falling to pieces: bricks had toppled from the chimney-stacks, spiders had spun their webs everywhere, and one might expect to find a brother to dragons in the great halls. "To live in it?" asked Mary. "Why, the very thing! Let the creepers cover all the main part and hold it up with their strong ropes if need be. But there in the east wing the rooms are reasonable. You have such a knack with carpentry and machines and things, you could turn that long window into a door, we could bolt off the main part--and--and there we are!"

"It is God-given!" said the lover. "But would you not be afraid of ghosts? This is a place to be known of these shadowy people."

"I would give anything to see one!" she exclaimed, and then began to shiver as if fearing to be taken at her word. Her hair had fallen down in her struggles with bushes and boughs and briers on the way up; she was braiding it in a shining rope of gold.

"It will grow and shroud you in gold in your grave," he said, passing a tress of it across his lips.

The color mounted in her cheeks, exquisite as that on a rose-petal; nothing could be more the opposite of ghostliness than she, the very picture of vital strength.

All at once it seemed to the poet that here was a way to put fresh being into this dead place, to suspend its decay, till it gathered force and new meaning and became instead of a suspected apparition a thing glowing with life. He went to the window and looked in; it gave way under his hand, and he stepped across. "This shall be the door," he said.

"And this the living-room," she replied. And they went through the wing.

"It is quite ample enough," he exclaimed.

"More than enough," she said.

"It will do very well," he continued. "I will come up with old Will and brooms and pails, and clear out the dust and cobwebs and litter, and mop and scour. I can do it."

"And I can help. Oh, how I can help!"

"Here will be your sewing-room. Here will be my writing-room--only you will sit there, too. Here is our own room. How fine a great fire roaring up this chimney will be! Here can be pantry and kitchen. See-- there is water running from some spring higher up the hill. It is really quite perfect. Why did we never think of it before? No one claims it. We shall be married now the moment it is ready to receive a bride. A fine place, those great halls, for children to romp in. I hear them now with their piping silver voices!"

"And I will have a garden on this side, with rows of lilies, with rows of roses, with white sweet-william against blue larkspur, with gillyflowers and pansies--oh, why didn't we think of this before!"

"We will need some furnishing--"

"Not a great deal. Mother and father will give us things they don't use. And we can make tables and dressers--you can."

"And I shall be paid for my verses the Magazine of Light accepted, some time."

"And there is the old automobile--though I don't know if I would like to ride in that, even if I could."

"I think I can furbish it up. I'll take a look at it. I always had a way with tools. Oh, yes, you will like to ride in it. It won't be quite--the same--may need some new parts."

"But--the poor Mad Lady--won't we be afraid?"

"Of what? She wouldn't hurt us if she could, and she couldn't if she would. She will be glad to have her limousine give pleasure to a young wife and her adoring man-at-arms. Oh, Mary, we have a home! But it's too good to be true. Come, let us hurry down before the whole thing fades like a dream!"

The parson and the schoolmaster and Mr. Ditton all went up the next day to look over the possibilities, and they all agreed that the plan was feasible. "The main building," said the schoolmaster, "could be used for a boarding-school," and he pictured himself a delighted headmaster there in no time.

"A fine place for one of those retreats where people invite heaven into their souls," said the parson.

"A place for much revelry unseen by the curious. I wonder it has not been utilized," said Mr. Ditton. And then they all did their kind best to help the poet and his sweetheart.

It was the prettiest wedding under the sun. All the village took note, and part of the people followed the pleasant procession up the hill. They had turned out in a body two or three weeks before and made the path up the hill wide and smooth; and all the furnishings and belongings had been taken up some days ago. The bridegroom, dark and straight, prouder that morning than if the Iliad had been his achievement, walked with his wife who, a little pale, found some strength in leaning on his arm, her veil flowing about her, half veil, half scarf, the rose in her hair the beginning of a long garland of roses that the school-children had braided for her, that fell on her shoulder and trailed to her feet. A group of the children followed, marshalled by the schoolmaster, all prettily demure, but full of the suspended spirit of gambol and outcry. Then came the glad young friends and companions, and next them the parson and his wife, solemn as if they were ascending the mount of sacrifice, which indeed they were doing in giving their child to an almost unknown man. After these came all who wished them well sufficiently to climb the steep; while the music of a flute-blower went all the way along from the sheltering wood.

A passing cloud obscured the main building, but the sun lay full on the east wing, which seemed to give a smiling welcome. On the terrace was a fine banquet spread, and a wedding-cake for the bride to cut; and after the dainties had been enjoyed and Billy Biggs's pockets stuffed as full as his stomach, and the flute-blower had come out of the wood, they all swarmed through the east wing and over the great house; and the schoolmaster formed a class there and told them in his own way the story of a wedding where one of the guests, a person of deific quality, had turned jars of water into wine. "That," said he, "is what marriage does. It gives to those who have drunk only water the wine of life." It is to be doubted if the little people understood him, but the poet did.

After this came dancing; and presently sunset was casting ruby fires over all the world. And the old parson went to the new husband and wife, and blessed them as if all power were given him to bless, and he kissed them both, and led the way home.

Then Mary went inside and divested herself of her lovely finery, and made the tea, and they supped together, and then sat on the door-stone and watched the moon come up and silver the great morass in the distance; and at last they went inside, and the husband locked the door. "Oh," said Mary, "when I heard you turn the key I knew that we had left the world outside!"

"And that you and I are one!" said her husband.

The poet did not do much with his epic, after all, that year; but he gave us that charming masque of "Mornings in Arcady" that haunts its lovers as remembered strains of music do. And he made the beginnings of his wife's garden, and he wrought with his carpentry tools, and did some repairing on the motor-car; sooth to say, it needed a good deal of renewing, and it took all the amount of the check for his poem to replace the useless parts, and from other verses, too.

And by and by came the little child, as if a small angel had wandered out of heaven. And Mary began to have a strange foreboding about the main building, as of some baleful influence there that might harm the child. So her husband took the child with her and went all over the main building, and showed her there was nothing there but emptiness, not even gloom; for how could gloom live in a place flooded with sunshine through all its many windows? After the twin babies came, Mary had the clothes hung there to dry.

Sometimes now they had the flute-blower come up, and all their friends from the village, to make merry in the spacious places of the main building, which seemed to put on a brighter face in welcome. And again, when there was rumor of war the women gathered there to scrape lint and roll bandages, while their children played about. Sometimes in summer the Sunday-school received their lessons there and sang their hymns, and had their festa. And the poet had his wish of seeing his children at play there. Once in a while the visiting village children found themselves storm-bound there, staying for days together, and the wide rooms rang with their glad voices. The place was full of life.

One day when her mother was there, the poet came to his wife, heralded by a great puffing and blowing, sliding to the door in the motor-car. "It is quite regenerated," he said. "I have run it down the road and back to make assurance doubly sure. Now mother will keep the babies, and we will follow the poor Mad Lady's way. Oh, I have had motors before. I could have them again if I chose to accept the conditions."

"Oh, I shall be afraid!" she said.

"Of what?" he asked, as he had asked before. "The machine is all right. Shabby, but can go like blazes. A pity I had not attended to it when we first set up our gods here. What a thing it is to have a wife!" as she obediently took her seat.

"What a thing it is to have a limousine," she answered, "and a chauffeur!"

As the car slid along Mary idly took up the speaking-tube through which one gives orders to the man outside. It seemed to her that she heard murmurs in it like a voice. At first faint, then the murmurs swelled till they were not only distinct but startling. Mary dropped the tube, but caught it up again, and put it to her ear. It was a woman's voice evidently. "Down this way," it seemed to say. "No, no, try the first turn to the left. Oh, did I say the left? I mean the right. Don't go by it! Now, straight ahead. Oh, stop, stop, let me think--this is not right! The Springwood way, the Commoners, now the third from the forks. Why should it be so difficult to reach the road where they bring in the hay? Oh, shall we never arrive? Shall we never find it? It might be lost! It might be water-soaked! It is at the roots of the big tree that leans over the marsh. Oh, here, here! Put on more speed! Hurry, hurry, faster! It is precious, it is priceless, lives depend upon it!"

It was Mary's turn to try to say "Stop!" But she could not bring herself to use that speaking-tube. She flung herself against the glass between herself and her husband. He turned and saw her terror, and stopped instantly. "What is it, what is it?" he cried. "Oh, Mary, what is the matter?"

"The car is haunted! By the Mad Lady's voice!" she exclaimed. "I hear it in the tube there! Oh, it is dreadful!"

"Nonsense, my darlingest! It is the wind you hear. Let me try it. I hear nothing. You see we are not moving now."

"Then move!" cried Mary, "and put your ear where you would hear me if I used it. I will go and sit with you."

She did so, and he reseated himself, and the car moved on, and the poet listened. "By George, it is saying something," he exclaimed presently. "'The third from the forks.' Why, that is just where we are. 'It is such a small thing it might be lost.' By George, Mary, what does this mean? There it goes again, 'Speed, hurry, hurry, it is precious, it is priceless, lives depend--' This is the weirdest thing I ever came across," he said, as he wiped his forehead. "Look here, suppose we obey the directions, go where she says and see what will happen?"

Mary was trembling in every limb; her teeth chattered, but she tried not to have it seen. They began to go forward, turning the corner, coming out on the straight road to the marsh.

It was a season of low tides, and except for a short but terrific thunder-storm there had been no rain for weeks, so that the marsh had visibly shrunk. "There's no danger, we won't go out on the marsh, of course. That chauffeur, the Mad Lady's, must have lost control, he was going at such a horrific rate, they say."

"There is the big tree on the edge!" cried Mary, still in a tremor, her very voice shaking.

"Let us look. We will find some sticks and turn up the earth," said her husband.

"Oh, it is the most awful thing!" murmured Mary. "I feel as if we were meddling in some terrible conspiracy, as if--as if--"

"As if the Prince of the Powers of the Air had it in for you. Never fear, sweetheart, I'm here."

He worked out the foot-rest of the car and began to break with it the soil about the roots of the tree. And then he saw that the earth had been torn up by a thunderbolt fallen there not long since, stripping the bark off the tree, too, but making his work more easy.

"There's nothing there at all!" cried Mary. "It's all our imagination."

"There's nothing like effort," he replied. "Aha, what is this?" And there resounded a slight metallic clang, and he wrenched out and brought to light a small japanned box covered with rust and mould.

"It may contain a fortune in priceless stones," he said.

"She said it was priceless," Mary answered. But they had nothing with which to open it; and he turned the car and they went home, feeling as if they had a weight of lead with them.

The parson had come up for his wife, and was as interested as Mary and the poet. It took only a few minutes with a chisel to open the box. Inside was a fast-locked ebony casket. "It is too bad to break it," said Mary.

"There is nothing else to do," he said, prying it open. They found then a lock of curling hair, a slender gold ring, and a piece of thin parchment on which was written something illegible, neither name nor place being decipherable, but yet which had an air of marriage lines.

"Now what does this mean?" asked the poet. "A house takes shape out of the air apparently, a woman lives in it, and drives round wildly in search of this box that has perhaps been stolen from her, whose contents were needed to prove innocence, descent, rights to property, and what-not, and loses her life searching for it. We must get out of this, Mary! The whole thing is a baseless fabric and will melt away, and for all I know melt us with it."

The schoolmaster and Mr. Ditton coming up on their afternoon stroll in which they usually discussed points of the cabala, had heard the poet's words. "You are doubting the stability of the house?" said the schoolmaster. "You need not. It is written in the Zohar that thought is the source of all that is, and searching the Sephiroth we find that matter is only a form of thought. In fact the soul builds the body--"

"Many a castle in the air has been made solid by putting in the underpinning," said Mr. Ditton.

"My children," said the parson, "if the Mad Lady was able to project herself and her palace to this spot, for reasons of her own, you have projected into it yourselves. Your innocent and happy lives have filled it with vitality, and have fixed a dream into a home. It is as strong as the foundations of the earth. Stay here in safety, the house and the home are permanent. The poor Mad Lady! Come, wife."

But Mary was still trembling a little.

THE END